Dear Reader:

LOVESWEPT celebrates he̶̶̶̶̶ who sweep us off our feet, who tantalize us with whispered endearments, and who challenge us with their teasing humor and hidden vulnerability. Whether they're sexy roughnecks or dashing sophisticates, dark and danger-ous or blond and brash, these men are heartthrobs, the kind no woman can get enough of. And now, just in time for Valentine's Day, all six books in this month's line-up have truly special covers that feature only these gorgeous heartthrobs. HEARTTHROBS—heroes who'll leave you spellbound as only real men can, in six fabulous new romances by only the best in the genre.

Don't miss any of our HEARTTHROBS this month

#528 A MAGNIFICENT AFFAIR by Fayrene Preston
#529 CALL ME SIN by Jan Hudson
#530 MR. PERFECT by Doris Parmett
#531 LOVE AND A BLUE-EYED COWBOY
       by Sandra Chastain
#532 TAKEN BY STORM by Tami Hoag
#532 BRANDED by Linda Warren

There's no better way to celebrate the most romantic day of the year than to cuddle up with all six LOVESWEPT HEARTTHROBS!

With best wishes,

Nita Taublib

Nita Taublib
Associate Publisher/LOVESWEPT

WHAT ARE *LOVESWEPT* ROMANCES?

They are stories of true romance and touching emotion. We believe those two very important ingredients are constants in our highly sensual and very believable stories in the *LOVESWEPT* line. Our goal is to give you, the reader, stories of consistently high quality that may sometimes make you laugh, sometimes make you cry, but are always fresh and creative and contain many delightful surprises within their pages.

Most romance fans read an enormous number of books. Those they truly love, they keep. Others may be traded with friends and soon forgotten. We hope that each *LOVESWEPT* romance will be a treasure—a "keeper." We will always try to publish

LOVE STORIES YOU'LL NEVER FORGET
BY AUTHORS YOU'LL ALWAYS REMEMBER

The Editors

Sandra Chastain
Love and a
Blue-eyed Cowboy

BANTAM BOOKS

NEW YORK · TORONTO · LONDON · SYDNEY · AUCKLAND

LOVE AND A BLUE-EYED COWBOY

A Bantam Book / March 1992

If you would be interested in receiving protective vinyl covers for your Loveswept books, please write to this address for information:

> *Loveswept*
> *Bantam Books*
> *P.O. Box 985*
> *Hicksville, NY 11802*

ISBN 0-553-44135-3

Published simultaneously in the United States and Canada

PRINTED IN THE UNITED STATES OF AMERICA

OPM   0 9 8 7 6 5 4 3 2 1

For Beth de Guzman, who understands about fragile egos and provides the enthusiasm and confidence that makes a relationship work. Thanks.

One

The woman was riding a pink bicycle, for Pete's sake, heading toward a gang of the toughest motorcycle buffs since the Hell's Angels.

Hunter Kincaid caught his breath, then let out a sigh of relief as he watched her pedal past the entrance to the motorcycle dealership. He leaned against a concrete pylon, adjusted his aviator sunglasses, and let his gaze slide back across the mass of humanity. They reminded him of buzzards circling a fresh road kill.

Banners strung across the parking area announced the scavenger hunt being held by the manufacturer of the new Panther Motorcycle as part of an introductory advertising campaign. But the fifty thousand dollars in prize money didn't entirely account for the crowd. This crew of road hogs would have been there for the prize of a new Panther cycle alone, Hunter surmised.

The same scenario was taking place in six other towns in the country. Fourteen teams of one man and one woman were to be selected in each area. A couple of hundred wide-eyed innocents mixed uneasily with the tough guys waiting for the drawing to select the teams to begin. Though he'd ridden with the best of them, even Hunter had never seen so much leather and so many tattoos in one place.

Mary Poppins on a pink bicycle didn't fit into that crowd.

Idly, Hunter chewed on a small brown cigar and wondered what had happened to her. He bent his knee and felt the ever-present ache in his lower back as he propped his foot against the concrete. He was tired of listening to the president of Panther, Inc., rave over the virtues of the motorcycle.

His gaze was drawn back to the sidewalk in search of the pink bicycle and its rider.

Across the parking area, Fortune Dagosta parked her bicycle in a stand of pines and hurried down the grass embankment, afraid they'd already started calling names. She'd learned only an hour earlier that Joe had filled out an entry form in her name. She was late. She was always late. Only this time she couldn't afford to be.

Joe, the oldest member of the group of orphans and runaways she'd taken in, had been gone when she'd awakened. But his note, the note she'd found pinned to her purse, had explained that when the organizers of the scavenger hunt called out her name, she had to be there, or she'd lose her chance at winning fifty thousand dollars. That was all she knew. She'd worry about the details later.

The temperature in Cordele, Georgia, was at least 95 degrees, and the concrete at two o'clock in the afternoon was hot enough to fry eggs on.

Fortune danced barefoot across the parking area as she skirted the crowd, trying to get closer to the platform. She couldn't imagine what had happened to her shoes. Misplacing things was nothing new to her, but she didn't want to think that Joe's being gone had anything to do with her missing tennis shoes. Still, she had a bad feeling about the connection.

The man standing at the bottom of the steps in the shadow of the second-story entrance to the building was out of Fortune's line of vision. She didn't see him grind out the cigar, flicking the hot ashes across the pavement. She only felt the fire burning the bottom of her left foot.

"Holy hell! I'm branded!" She let out a more vivid oath and hopped around, holding her injured foot crossed over her upper thigh.

Hunter Kincaid, leaning against the building, took a step toward her and shook his head. "That's not all you're going to be if you don't put on some shoes."

For the briefest moment their gazes met, and he felt an unexpected intensity of feeling arc between them. He couldn't seem to tear his gaze away from her face, a pert face with wide lips that were parted, not in anticipation of a kiss, but in fury.

"Well, thank you very much for your concern, Mr. Wise Guy." She glanced down at the ground, catching sight of the scattered ashes and the still-smoking cigar butt. "I don't suppose you know who threw that down."

"I did."

Fortune slowed her hopping and glared at the man who was frowning at her. His clothes were trendy and expensive. He hadn't pulled his designer jeans from the throwaway bag at the thrift shop. The boots certainly weren't hand-me-downs either. They were snakeskin probably, and the skin hadn't been long off the snake.

If that weren't enough, he was wearing a cowboy hat with a band that matched his boots. The Stetson was pushed to the back of his head, revealing a mass of sun-streaked blond hair. For a moment she had an insane urge to run her fingers through his thick locks. Yep, this sidewalk cowboy was well-heeled and full of himself, she determined, and runaway-from-home-with good-looking.

So what if he did set off skyrockets in her stomach? she told herself. What gave him the right to pollute the earth and contaminate the ground where innocent people could blister their feet? He didn't have to lay down a bed of fire to burn her; he was roasting her with the intensity of his gaze.

"You did that? Why?"

"Well, I didn't expect company," said Hunter, not caring for the sudden coil of heat that fired in his lower body. The woman probably didn't weigh a hundred pounds soaking wet. Sizzling dark eyes glared at him as if he were the enemy. His first impression of her as a *Sesame Street* follower ended when he glimpsed those flashing black eyes. Where she belonged was in some MTV rock video.

Except for the freckles, he thought, the freckles didn't fit the punk image. They weren't covered with makeup. They were just there, a peach-color scattering of freckles below the darkest, most expressive eyes he'd ever seen—eyes that were exploding with pent-up anger. She seemed as confused over what was happening as he, but while she covered her uncertainty with fury, he covered his with stoic indifference. Hunter decided that they were both very good at shielding their emotions.

Decked out in jeans with no knees and a hairdo that resembled a frightened porcupine, she stood her ground. Her looks matched her personality— outrageous. Normally, he'd just walk away, but something about those freckles challenged him. And being challenged by a freckle-faced, fire-breathing pixie was a welcome change from dealing with the perky, charming "And how are we feeling today, Mr. Kincaid?" attitude of the nurses who'd driven him mad for the last twelve weeks.

The strange cut of her short, spiked hairdo and the *Down with the Establishment* on her T-shirt told Hunter that he was doing battle with a woman who had no qualms about taking on causes, and at the moment the cause was him. She was bound to be one of those fanatics who didn't eat meat and would attack him for contaminating her airspace.

Still, he shouldn't have wounded her. He was out of practice with apologies, but he was about to try when she railed at him.

"Okay, Mr. Big Shot. You've made your statement. It's your space, and I invaded it. You don't care much about other people, do you?"

Fortune didn't know why she was behaving so badly. Normally, she was easygoing. It had to be this man who gave the impression of a powder keg, contained but ready to explode at any minute, who forced her to act so out of character.

"Not much," he drawled, pleased to see her register shock at his honesty. "I've found the feeling pretty much mutual. Are you always this prickly?"

Fortune's feet really hurt now, both of them. The sun had cooked the sidewalk to a red-hot intensity. She glanced around, seeking shade. There was none.

"I'm not prickly. I'm in pain. The least you could do is step aside and let me share your shade," she said. "I mean, I think you owe it to me since you're responsible for my injury."

"Certainly." Hunter stepped sideways, allowing Fortune to move into the small shady space. They were too close, he thought. He could smell an elusive floral scent, like wildflowers in the spring.

Damn, he must not be as strong as he'd thought. Maybe all those weeks in bed had affected his mind. Here he was thinking of hidden meadows and wood sprites, sprites with bare feet and freckles. He stood there for a moment, then said, "I'm sorry that you were burned."

"It's my fault, actually. I ought not to be barefoot, but you ought not to be smoking. Both things are bad for the health, cowboy."

Her tongue slipped out from between her lips, painting them with moisture in the heat. As Hunter stared down at her, he had the absurd desire to follow the path her tongue had taken with his own.

Maybe it was the heat that was making him crazy. He shook his head, trying to focus on his reason for being there, the chance at a spot on the scavenger-hunt team.

"The name's Hunter, and do you always tell other people what they should do?"

"Yes." She glanced up at him, her eyes bright

with merriment. "Hmmm, Hunter. As in bounty hunter?"

"I've been called that."

The name fit. "Do you take your victims back alive?"

"I haven't lately."

"That's about what I thought." She pulled her shirttail down and dusted off the bottom of her foot, muttering under her breath, "There was a young woman with bare feet, who burned them— bleep, bleep. The devil from hell, gave orders very well, but the dude was basically cheap."

"I'm sorry, what did you say?"

"Nothing. I was making up a limerick. Forget it."

"Look, I really am sorry about your feet. I don't normally singe my victims. As soon as the drawing is over, I'll make it up to you by buying you a new pair of shoes and a shirt."

"No thanks, I'll survive." She glanced at the shirt and grimaced. "No need to replace the shirt, I didn't buy it. It came from Goodwill. I guess you don't do much shopping there, Mr. Hunter."

"Not Mr. Hunter, it's Hunter Kincaid. And I haven't shopped there lately, but I know of them." He could have said he knew of them well, but he didn't, adding instead, "Where are your shoes, anyway?"

Hunter didn't even know why he'd given her his name. It connected them somehow, and that was the last thing he wanted. She reminded him of one of his grandmother's fancy chickens, ready to peck the hand of anybody trying to take the eggs from her nest.

Hunter squinted and wondered why on earth he'd remembered his grandmother. She'd been dead for twenty years. And although he missed her, he knew a woman who cooked on an old black iron stove and drew her water from a well would never fit into a modern world where the offspring she'd produced wore tuxedos and ate truffles and cherries flambé.

"I couldn't find my shoes this morning."

She could have explained about the fire that had burned all her clothes and nearly ended her attempt to provide a haven for runaway kids, but that was her business. There'd been enough publicity about a homeless kid named Joe who'd almost destroyed a local landmark. "I was told that if I wasn't here when they called my name, I wouldn't qualify for a spot in the scavenger hunt— I had to leave without them."

Hunter didn't even try to conceal his surprise. "You only just found out about the drawing? You do know those chosen are expected to leave tomorrow? What kind of work do you do that you can take off at the drop of a hat?"

"I'm a housekeeper. I work for a cleaning service as a fill-in when one of the regular crew members can't make it."

He took off his sunglasses and studied her.

Fortune didn't know anything about the rules. But her fervent "I'll be ready" was half-swallowed as she got lost in the blue of the cowboy's eyes.

Hunter Kincaid's eyes weren't shaped any differently from anyone else's. They weren't that much larger, or that much bluer, but somehow, all put together and crowned by thick eyebrows that framed them perfectly, the effect of his eyes was as unexpected as primroses in the snow or a colored stone on the bottom of a mountain stream.

"Where's your partner?" Hunter couldn't wait to see who had teamed up with a barefoot woman who spouted limericks.

Fortune swallowed hard. She was beginning to figure out that there were other things that Joe hadn't explained to her. "Ah, I'm not sure."

"I hope he's a big, tough guy, because I have my doubts that you can handle one of those new Panther machines. Are you sure," he asked with an unexpected softness, "you know what you're doing?"

She wasn't at all sure, but she couldn't admit it. "I can do anything I need to do. How tough are you? From where I stand, those boots don't have a scuff on them." His blue eyes narrowed; his muscles were rigid with tension. The fire on the bottom of her feet seemed to move upward at an alarming rate.

"You have no idea how tough I am, or how far I've traveled in these boots."

This time there was pain in the cowboy's voice, and Fortune, always a sucker for somebody who was hurting, regretted her outburst. She'd never walked in his shoes, and therefore shouldn't judge his actions.

She blinked, trying to close off the shattering intensity of his gaze while she searched for something to say, and settled for the truth.

"I'm sorry," she said softly. "Where's your partner?" she asked, curious abut the woman he'd chosen.

"I'm wondering about that myself." Hunter glanced at his watch, grateful for the distraction. The woman he'd asked had been a friend, someone he knew well enough to travel with for nine days, no strings attached.

"What happens if she doesn't show up?" Fortune's question was more important than he could guess.

"I forfeit my chance at the money."

Uh-oh. If she had to have a partner, she was sunk. Joe hadn't mentioned that in the note. Fortune glanced around, trying to spot a familiar face in the crowd, someone—anyone—whom she could coerce into being her partner.

The men listening to the speaker were all leather-clad strangers—tough-looking strangers. All except the man standing beside her. And he already had a partner.

Then the official drawing began. Hunter hoped that his partner was there somewhere, looking for him.

Fortune closed her eyes. She needed that money. She needed to have her name selected. She needed a partner.

Suddenly, she knew with breath-stopping certainty what was about to take place. They both happened to be in the same place at the same time—alone. His partner hadn't shown up, and she didn't have one. It was fate.

Still, she refused to concede the obvious until the president of Panther, Inc., pulled out thirteen entries that had neither Hunter's name on them nor hers. Then came the last selection: the Hunter Kincaid team.

Hunter looked around, scanning the crowd. There was no woman moving toward the platform. Something must have happened. Damn! He wasn't about to lose his spot. There was only one thing to do. He reached back and, taking Fortune by the arm, pulled her through the crowd like a rag doll, seeking as much shade as possible until he reached the platform steps.

"What are you doing, cowboy?" Fortune demanded.

"You wanted to go on a scavenger hunt. It looks like you've got your wish, *partner*."

"You're out of your mind."

"I probably am," he conceded as they reached the platform. "Smile," Hunter urged, "and try not to look so—so—wild."

On the stand Hunter identified himself to the official.

"And your partner?"

Hunter was caught short. He didn't even know the woman's name. He turned toward her in question.

"Fortune Dagosta," she answered, returning his gaze with daggers in hers.

The hunt director motioned for them to take their place beside the other teams and went on with his instructions. "Tomorrow morning the teams will assemble here. You will receive your instructions and your clues. Today I just want to caution you about the rules."

Hunter listened, wondering if he'd made a mistake. But he was flat broke and determined not to be more obligated to his family than he already was. After the bike accident he hadn't wanted to go from the hospital to his family home, but he'd had little choice. He'd known what that would mean, what his adoptive father, Hale Kincaid, would say.

"Hunter, Son, when are you going to quit wasting time racing motorcycles and settle down?

Kincaid Industries is growing. You know, I had hoped that you'd take an interest in the hotels. That's the division I envisioned for you to head."

"I can't," he'd tried to explain. "I don't fit in— cities are too confining," he'd added. "I need to be free to—"

"You'd rather be a bum than take what I'm offering you," Hale Kincaid had repeated, just as he'd done over and over during the nearly twenty-five years since he'd married Hunter's mother. "You can't be serious about living in that run-down fishing camp your grandfather called a resort."

"I am," Hunter said, "and I will. Grandfather left the camp to me, and I intend to reopen it. That's all I want."

Words had been spoken in anger, but Hunter had to make Hale understand that he meant them. He wasn't a real Kincaid. He was the adopted son, the outsider, the reminder of his mother's past, with a background that his adoptive father wanted desperately to obliterate.

But the fishing camp, nestled on the bank of the Flint River, was falling down. The wonderful screened-in shed where he remembered his grand-mother cooking fresh fish was a dirt-floored build-ing with half a roof and the screen hanging in tatters.

Registering for the scavenger hunt had seemed a good idea. Winning the prize was the quickest way to finance his plan now that bike racing was off-limits. But his plan to claim the entire prize was being threatened by a smart-mouthed half-pint with kissable lips and peach-colored freckles— the worst possible partner.

"Better listen, cowboy," his teammate said. "I think these instructions apply to you too."

"You'll be furnished with camping gear, vouchers for gas, and five thousand dollars in cash to be used any way you choose, except to pay for outside assistance. Your mode of travel will be limited to your Panther. Your partner is the only person allowed to view your map or study your clues."

"Can we stop along the way? What about the Burger Doodle? Is that a no-no?" somebody called out from the rear.

"Because the point of this scavenger hunt is to introduce a tough new machine that will take you to the outback of Australia, you are being provided with camping equipment and food. But the Panther is a city machine as well. Therefore, commercial comforts are not against the rules," the director announced with a quirky smile. "Provided you stay within your monetary allotment."

The second official picked up when the first one stopped. "You may not make use of any personal effects, monies, or credit cards. Please pick up your supplies, choose your machine, and mark it with the proper team number. You will assemble at nine A.M. to draw your clues. Use your imagination and ingenuity. And good luck."

"Well, wild woman, I hope you have an imagination and that you're not going to fold on me."

"The imagination is fine," Fortune said with the beginnings of a guilty conscience. Now that she'd been chosen, she was starting to have a nagging attack of self-doubt. "It's the other . . . mechanical skills I have to brush up on."

"That you don't have to worry about. If there's

anything I'm an expert at, it's keeping a bike operational."

"It isn't the mechanics I'm worried about," Fortune confessed, "it's the motorcycle. Could I see one—up close?"

"You mean you've never even seen the new Panther? It's one mean machine. I can't wait to try it out."

Fortune only swallowed hard. She tried hard not to look as if she were sorry she'd been chosen. She had the feeling that the woman she was replacing was a real motorcycle buff.

"Neither can I," she said as she followed the cowboy across the platform. But her bravado died when she saw what she was expected to ride. It was big and black and looked like one of those robo-monsters from the cartoons. She expected it to lean back and roar.

"What do you think?" Hunter walked over and ran his long fingers lovingly across the handlebar.

The look on Hunter's face was one of passion, of desire. Fortune shivered. For one quick second she wondered how it would feel to have him react like that to her. She'd been wrong; Hunter wasn't the powder keg, she was—and she wasn't certain that the fuse hadn't already been lit.

"Well?" Hunter invited her to move closer.

She looked at the motorcycle. She couldn't move. Her feet were glued to the wooden platform floor. She'd have to spend the night there, standing up, waiting for her secret to be discovered. She closed her eyes and prayed for help. She didn't know who the saint of motorcycles was, but she settled on Saint Christopher, begging for intervention, for divine inspiration.

What she got was reality.

"Fortune Dagosta. That's really your name?"

"Yes. I'm named for my Spanish great-great-great-great-great-grandmother. She stowed away in a ship and sailed to Mexico, where she met my Italian treasure-hunting grandfather."

Hunter shook his head. "I don't know why I asked. I don't know why I expected your answer to make any sense."

"I don't even know if the story is true. Somebody probably made it up. The Dagostas have always been known for their imagination and their need to travel."

"Like you, I suppose," Hunter said. His observation of his partner so far confirmed those characteristics. The woman certainly had an imagination. "You're about to spend nine days traveling around with a stranger."

"Yeah, it won't be the first time." Her father had spent most of his life traveling with strangers, from one tenant farm to another. As a young child, Fortune had often been left to fend for herself.

A kid had to grow up fast when her parents were migrant workers who never stayed in one place longer than a month. When her mother had died, her father had dumped her with Granny Dagosta. Fortune's life hadn't changed much, it had just expanded. Later, when she'd lit out on her own, she'd been prepared to survive.

Catching the odd expression on Hunter's face, Fortune quickly added, "I've done a lot of moving around." She knew that she hadn't answered his question about strangers, but he didn't press the issue. Taking a chance on someone she didn't know had become a way of life for Fortune. Trusting Hunter Kincaid was a small risk to take for the prize. Besides, she was quick, and she did have a good imagination. Fortune Dagosta could look after herself. She always had.

"So be it," Hunter finally said, resigned to spending the next nine days with a woman with multi-color hair and a blistered foot. "You want to pick up the supplies, or choose our bike?"

"The supplies," Fortune said quickly. "The bike is your department." That statement was more true than Hunter Kincaid could possibly know.

Twenty minutes later Fortune had two bedrolls, an instant camera, film, a first-aid kit, and two packages of goods that she was told would fit into the storage compartments that lay like a saddle across the back of the bike. She carried the supplies to the spot beneath the steps where she'd met Hunter, and waited.

Another half hour went by before the sun god in the Stetson walked stiffly back down the steps to where she was waiting.

"Since you're going to have to drive our machine, you need to check it out."

"Drive it?" This time Fortune couldn't keep the sheer terror from her voice.

"Tell me I'm not hearing what I think I am, partner."

"What do you think you're hearing?"

"Fear. I think I'm hearing fear. You do ride a bike, don't you?"

"Yes, that was probably a requirement, wasn't it?"

"It was. What kind of bike do you usually ride?"

"I—I—well," she stumbled around, trying to figure out how to confess her deception. "Of course I ride a bike. It's parked up by the trees. You can see it from here."

Hunter swung around and scanned the stand of pines. All he saw was the pink two-wheeler with the wicker basket on the handlebars, the bike powered by two silver pedals. Then he knew. Mary Poppins.

"Ahh no! Tell me that wasn't you riding that pink bicycle. He hadn't recognized her. She'd been too far away, a silhouette against the sun. "I don't believe it. Surely, you knew when you entered what kind of bike the Panther is. You couldn't mistake a motorcycle dealership with a bicycle shop. Why would you do that to me?"

"I told you, I didn't enter the contest myself." There was no point in telling him that Joe, who was only sixteen and probably ineligible, had planned to be her partner. "Someone else—a friend did it for me. I'm really sorry. Nobody told me that I'd have to drive it. I don't think I can. Those things scare me to death."

He was staring at her with eyes like steel marbles, totally demolishing her normal self-confidence. And she was rattling on like an idiot—just as she always did when she was uncertain.

"Ah, hellfire," she swore. "There was a woman from Cordele, who possibly screwed up the deal. She said she could ride, but the truth is she lied. Boy does she feel like a heel."

Hunter Kincaid couldn't decide whether he felt more like hitting her or kissing her. But both possibilities were cut off when a sudden spasm of pain zipped up his spinal cord and pinched off his breathing for a second. He waited until it passed, then realized that she was staring at him. From the look on her face he couldn't tell whether she was afraid of his anger or ashamed of her lie. Either way it was too late to do anything about it. The crowd had dispersed, and if he went to the officials about the mistake now, he'd be dropped from the competition.

Besides, she was getting to him. For a man who traveled alone, he didn't understand his protective feelings for this wild woman." He rationalized that it was because she was his only hope of winning the money. He couldn't blame her. If she hadn't been around, he'd have been out of the competition.

"Poetry? Bad poetry? In the middle of a crisis. Why not? It fits."

"Sorry, it's a habit. I make up rhymes when I'm nervous."

Hunter simply shook his head and repeated Fortune's earlier oath as he knelt down on the ground in front of where she was sitting. "Give me your foot?"

"Why, is this something kinky?"

"I'm going to put medication on those burns."

Fortune stared in amazement as he opened the first-aid kit, pulled out a gauze pad, and wiped off the bottom of her foot. Next he applied antiseptic ointment and a Band-Aid.

"You'd better clean that up when you get home," he said, and reached over to pick up the boxes at her feet. Reaching down was all he could do; he couldn't begin to lift them. "Ahh!"

"What's wrong, Kincaid?"

Hunter gritted his teeth and forced himself to ignore the pain as he stood. "Looks like you're going to have to carry the supplies, wild woman. I seem to be having a little lifting problem."

"You are in pain, aren't you? I thought so."

"Just a minor problem with my spinal cord. It will pass, but I'm not supposed to lift anything for a few more days." A lot more, actually. Actually, he wasn't even supposed to be riding a bike yet.

"Not lift?" She eyed him seriously. The man was in more than a little pain, yet he'd stopped to treat hers. She couldn't figure him out. She already knew that he would never have admitted he couldn't lift unless it was a real problem. She was beginning to understand his slow walk and the stiff way he stood. "You're hurt, aren't you?"

"Not anymore."

"I don't think I believe that. How did you get here?"

"I drove my truck."

"But I thought you were a bike rider."

"I am, but mine has been in the shop."

She took two steps forward until she was standing directly in front of him. Standing as tall as she could, she said, "From an accident, no doubt."

When he didn't speak, she knew she had her answer. "Great! I can't drive a motorcycle, and you're hurt. Hellfire, what a team we're going to be. And I need that money! Didn't the entry form ask if you were in good physical condition?"

"It did. It also asked if the person entering was an experienced biker. What did your helpful friend say to that?"

"He said yes, and I am. For twenty of my twenty-six years I've been riding a bike. Nobody asked what kind."

"So what do we do now, wild woman?"

"What else?" she said forcefully. "We win! I *need* that money."

"What for?" he asked, but he wasn't sure he wanted to know, not when he'd intended from the beginning to claim it all.

"I need that money to fix the castle roof."

"Castle? Of course. Sure, that makes sense. You're Cinderella, and I'm Huck Finn."

Fortune started to protest. But the picture she'd conjured up of the two of them turned her protest into an impish smile. "Somehow you look about as much like Huck Finn as I do a princess. You don't even have a fishing pole."

Hunter watched her smile turn into laughter and change from an expression of relief to the real thing, genuine and contagious. "Where're your glass slippers?" He heard himself responding, and for a moment they simply laughed at the absurdity of the situation, until his sore back forced him to stop.

Finally, Fortune realized that he'd grown quiet. She took a deep breath and raised her eyes. "Looks like we're stuck with each other, cowboy. Two people out of a bad joke. I'm sorry, but as you may already have guessed, I'm no Cinderella. I don't do sculleries."

"Well, if you're looking for a prince, you're out of luck. What you got is a frog, warts and all."

And then she knew. Everything was going to be all right. They were a pair of misfits—very different from each other, but both out of step somehow with the rest of the world. They had been matched and they'd win.

"Maybe," she said with a growing confidence in her voice. "But you remember that the frog turned into a prince. If I hand you a couple of these boxes, can you carry them?"

Hunter couldn't think of a snappy reply. He remembered the fairy tale. It took a kiss from the princess to do the job, and at the moment that was all he could think about. He was going squirrelly. He was nodding his head.

Hunter found himself striding across the parking lot with the last person on earth he would have picked as a partner. He had no idea that he was still smiling until he reached the truck and caught a glimpse of his expression in the window. Quickly, he erased the grin, slid the boxes beneath the covered body of his pickup truck, took the bedrolls she was carrying, and shoved them inside. "Now, wild woman," he said more sharply than he intended, "get your bike."

"Why?"

"Listen, you barely got to the drawing in time to qualify. I already lost one partner, and I don't intend to take a chance on your being late and disqualifying us in the morning. Where do you live?"

"Why do you care where I live?"

"Because I'm spending the night with you."

Fortune swallowed her surprise. It was starting already. From the time she'd stepped on the cowboy's hot ashes, she'd known that something major was about to happen. She couldn't imagine why she was supposed to be there, but a long time ago she'd learned to roll with the punches. She'd made it through some pretty tough times alone. Her partner thought he needed to look after her. But it was probably the other way around, she thought.

He wanted to spend the night. Great! She'd let him. What better way for him to understand why she had to have the prize money. Yep, Fortune looked at the sky. A heat storm was building in the distance. Perfect!

By the time they turned down the gravel road to the house where Fortune lived, big wet drops were making dusty splotches on the windshield. By the time they dashed up on the porch, the rain was falling in torrents.

Hunter slung rainwater from the brim of his hat and took a good look at Fortune's house. She was right, she did need a new roof, and when she got that done, she needed to install a new house beneath it. The castle was falling down around its frame, the sad burned-out remains of what was once a grand old southern mansion. About the only solid part left of the structure was the porch they were standing on, and a swing jerking eerily back and forth in the storm.

"Now you see why I need the prize money."

Hunter shook his head. "I don't think twenty-five thousand dollars will be quite enough, Ms. Dagosta. I don't think that the whole prize would do it."

"I know," she admitted, staring at the structure with regret. "But I have to start somewhere. I have six kids depending on me."

"Six kids?" There was no way he could keep the disbelief from his voice. "You're kidding."

"At the moment. Who knows what the future will bring? There's probably another one due any time."

He stared at her for a long, disbelieving moment.

The sky opened up and sent another torrent of rain down on the roof.

"Damn!" Not only was his partner a black-eyed fantasy who threatened every ounce of self-control he could muster, she was pregnant too.

Two

"I'm not having a baby, cowboy. I'm not even married."

He fought back the acknowledgment of relief that welled up inside him. "The last time I checked, that wasn't exactly a prerequisite."

"For me it is. These children aren't mine, not biologically. But they're my responsibility, just the same. Don't you like children?"

"I don't know," Hunter said wearily. He was tired. His back ached, and his mind was spinning. He felt as if he'd just stepped off the Tilt-a-Whirl at the amusement park.

"Relax, Mr. Kincaid. Come with me. I'll introduce you to my kids. I think you'll understand." Fortune started off the porch and around the back of the house.

The rain was falling steadily, but the thick leaves of the umbrella-shaped chinaberry trees overhead sheltered them. Then they emerged from the trees and cut through a rose garden, where the bushes were hanging heavy with roses as large as cereal bowls.

The woman he was following was trouble. Hunter had known that the moment he'd seen her dancing barefoot across the concrete at the dealership. He was thirty-four years old, and the one thing he'd learned in his life was that a man who traveled alone had fewer complications. Children were complications for which he'd never give up his solitary life.

But he'd never envisioned giving up racing either. He'd never planned to have an accident that would put him in the hospital and end his career as a dirt-track rider, but his life had been a series of unplanned changes, and now he was dealing with another—a body that was broken. His recovery wasn't progressing easily. The lingering pain of fused vertebrae had come as a surprise. Even as he splashed across the back drive, he felt the ever-present spasms and wondered why he was following Fortune Dagosta.

Fortune Dagosta. The name couldn't have been more perfect. The woman who held his immediate future in her hands was a flake, and yet all he could think about as he followed her was the way her hips moved and the way his muscles tightened in response.

She was tiny, and determined, and convinced that she was right. Just as his mother had been when she'd followed Hale Kincaid.

He'd never understood his mother's reasons either, no matter how hard she'd tried to explain. From the time his mother had married the man she'd worked for as his confidential secretary,

Hunter had tried every way he could to punish his wealthy adoptive father.

At ten years of age Hunter had resented the marriage and Hale. At thirty-four he still refused to believe that Hale Kincaid loved his mother. He believed Hale had married her to keep her quiet over some shady business deal or other, such as the one that forced men to work in an unsafe plant, the plant where his father had been killed.

Hale Kincaid might have adopted him, but Hunter still remembered his father's animosity toward his boss, remembered his father's claims that the man was more interested in his bank account than the safety of his workers. After his father had died, Hale Kincaid had tried to pretend he was a knight in shining armor, giving his mother a job, and two years later marrying her.

But Hunter had never forgiven him. He was his father's son, determined to go his own way. And he had—until now.

Hunter's foot slid for a second, and he righted himself, feeling the sharp pain he'd come to expect when he made a sudden move.

Fortune stopped and turned, catching a glimpse of pain in his eyes. She almost reached out to help him, caught herself, and waited. Maybe it was a mistake, bringing a man who was hurting into her life. She, who identified well with pain, was too drawn to the one who hurt.

She felt his eyes on her and followed the direction of his gaze. Her T-shirt was wet. It hugged her breasts like a spotlight, targeting nipples that, in spite of her best efforts, tightened as she watched.

Lifting his gaze to her face, Hunter felt a twinge of respect for her. The woman he was following didn't pretend. The awareness flowed between them, open and acknowledged. But, like him, she wouldn't let it interfere with whatever she was going after. He could understand that. Still, this children business didn't make sense.

"I guess I'd better know, Fortune. Is there a man in your life? I mean, the missing partner, maybe?"

The rain continued. They were standing there facing each other for he didn't know how long, when she finally answered.

"He's still missing. But there isn't *a* man in my life," she said. "There are four of them."

Fortune turned and walked the few steps to the barn. She opened the door, peering inside. "Hey, guys, are you in here?" She stepped inside and motioned for Hunter to follow.

"Yo, Fortune. Did you get picked?" A tall, lanky boy ambled into the center of the barn. He rocked back and forth on his heels as he studied Hunter.

"I did, thanks to you guys. Where is everybody?"

"After school they went into town with Lucy. You know how she is when a storm comes up. Head for cover and hide under the bed. I waited for you."

"Mickey, you shouldn't make fun of Lucy. You know that her house was struck by lightning when she was a child. Everybody in her family was killed in the fire except her. Mickey, this is Mr. Kincaid, my partner for the scavenger hunt. Hunter, Mickey."

"You're the one who entered Fortune in the contest?"

"No, it was Joe's idea. All I did was snitch the form. He filled it out and put it in the bowl."

"And how old is Joe?"

"Sixteen, same as me."

Hunter gave Fortune a puzzled look. "You travel with two sixteen-year-olds? And you were worried about me having a foot fetish."

"Not two, four," Fortune corrected with a grin. "Four boys and two girls. And we lived in Lucy's house."

"Not anymore," Mickey corrected. "Fortune, I know you're going to be upset, but I promised I wouldn't tell you. Joe took off this morning."

"Where'd he go?"

"All I could get out of him was that he wanted to check out the Hemingway cats."

"Oh, no." Now the note and a missing pair of shoes made sense. She should have figured it out that morning. She would have, if she hadn't been in such a hurry."

Joe was gone again. Joe, who had no home to run away from, seldom stayed in one place for long. He'd covered most of the East Coast in the last year. She'd never understood how he'd escaped being picked up by the authorities. He was so small that he looked like a child. She and Joe had a lot in common.

Watching, Hunter felt her crushing disappointment. He could actually see the pain reflected in her eyes. One of her children had left, and she was hurting. "What are Hemingway cats?" he asked.

Fortune straightened her shoulders and forced herself to answer. "Ernest Hemingway liked cats, and he had a pair with huge extra toes. When he

died, his house was sold to a local family. They've
preserved it as a museum. The owner of the house
loved the cats and kept them. The six- and seven-
toed animals kept reproducing and became known
as the Hemingway cats."

"Yeah, freak cats," Mickey said with a sneer,
"just like us. At least somebody provides food and
a home for those misfits."

"Ah, Mickey." Fortune put her arms around the
boy and hugged him. "I'll miss Joe too. But running away isn't the answer. Maybe—maybe he'll
find out that Florida doesn't have what he's looking for either. Maybe he'll come back."

Hunter watched as the tiny woman comforted
the boy who was already two heads taller than she.
Mickey bent and rested his chin on top of Fortune's head. Hunter couldn't tell which of them
was more upset, until Fortune backed away with a
sniff and wiped her eyes on her sleeve.

"Well, Mickey, if everybody else has gone into
town, we might as well get our clothes and join
them. No point in sleeping in the barn, cowboy,
when there are cots available."

"Cots? I'm afraid to ask where."

"Then don't. You wanted to spend the night with
me, let's hit the road. I'm hungry."

The rain had stopped. Mickey and Fortune fell
into step, and Hunter moved hesitantly along
behind them. What he wanted to do was drop
them somewhere and put the entire day out of
his mind. Fortune Dagosta wasn't just a wild
woman, she was a temptation, the kind of fantasy
that a man dreamed up in his most private
moments but avoided in real life. The random
thought of her in his bed flickered through his

mind with an unwelcome jolt. The last thing he wanted right now was a man-woman relationship with Fortune Dagosta.

He mentally ran through her undesirable characteristics again, imprinting them across his thoughts like a negative that had been overexposed. He immediately discounted the fiery black eyes that challenged him with every bat of her inch-long lashes, by focusing on her peaked hair. He replaced her perfect breasts and tight little bottom that was practically sending out "touch me" signals as she walked, with her "I dare you" attitude.

Try as he might, he couldn't do a thing about the freckles. Somehow, he couldn't erase the wild-woman image. She didn't make sense. He wasn't even certain that he liked her, but there was an unmistakable attraction between them that any other time would have made him turn and run. The fifty-thousand-dollar prize, however, made him swallow his reservations and follow.

After all, he reasoned, like her or not, the woman was his partner, and if he had any chance of winning the scavenger hunt, he had to find a way to use her to his best advantage. She had two redeeming characteristics: her determination and her wacky, offbeat mind. Maybe she could channel it into solving the puzzle.

Maybe.

Their destination was the last place he might have gone to search for four kids and a woman who was afraid of storms. It wasn't a summer camp, or a shelter for the homeless. The sign over the gate they were driving through—the pad-locked, guarded gate being closed behind them by a uniformed guard—read Crisp County Prison Farm.

"What kind of woman would take children from a burned-out house to a prison farm?"

"A true friend, cowboy. Tom Benson is the war-den. The children stay in his house. It's away from the compound, separated from the prisoners by a ten-foot wall. The kids are safer here than where they came from."

"Considering everything else that has happened today, I suppose you could say sleeping in a jail makes some kind of sense."

Hunter turned off the engine and opened the truck door. He blinked his eyes and mentally replayed his words. "I can't believe I said that."

Fortune had a feeling that Hunter would have preferred to be anyplace else in the world. There was something about the prison that bothered him. She could tell it by the strained expression on his face, by the way he hovered close to his truck, as though he expected to need it for a fast getaway.

"Tom's wife, Rachel, is with Child Welfare. She's the one who is trying to help us get our license to operate a temporary facility for runaways. She'd even agreed to be the resident counselor—until we had our little fire. She and Tom have plenty of room, and they've offered us a place to stay until we get all this worked out."

Inside the house the children were already bedded down for the night. Lucy was doing her schoolteacher bit, listening to them read from the dog-eared books that Fortune had rescued from the trash bins behind the elementary school. No matter that the four children doing the reading were long past third grade.

"Hi, Fortune, who's the dude?" The girl speaking was blond—at least the outer edges of her hair were blond. There was a streak down one side that was the same color as the barn behind the burned-out house.

"I should have known. Like mother, like daughter," Hunter muttered under his breath.

"Yep," Fortune agreed with a grin. "There was a woman from Umsters, who found a look-alike right in the dumpsters. They worked through the night, to make their hair a fright, and applied for jobs as twin Munsters."

"Phew, Fortune," the girl said, holding her nose in an exaggerated gesture of rejection.

"Okay, so my limericks lack something. You still have to admit they're original."

"Great!" Hunter said, "if having a partner dressed in quilt-scrap couturier isn't enough, she's a comedian too."

Fortune could have said that she was reasonably good at intuition and hunches, but from the confused look on her partner's face, she decided to stop the game-playing. He'd been a good sport up to now, and she owed him an explanation.

"Sorry, Hunter, let me introduce you. This is my friend Lucy. My look-alike is called Jade. We're not related, beyond a kindred spirit. You've already met Mickey. The others are Teddy, Carol, and Beau. They're friends, visitors. They're here temporarily."

"Yeah," Beau agreed, staring at Fortune's feet. "Visiting temporarily. I've been meaning to talk to you, Fortune. I didn't mind the house, but I'm not cut out for this kind of shelter. I'm thinking about moving on too."

Fortune sat down on a cot. "Oh, no, Beau. Not yet. You've only got three more weeks until the school year ends. Don't go." His revelation wasn't unexpected. It seemed that when one of her kids moved on, everybody else began to waver. She wanted them to find their way, but not by running away.

"Aw, Fortune, what good's that gonna do? I can't stay here. I need a job, and there ain't anybody gonna hire me. You just talking crap 'bout us having a normal life. Look what happened to Joe. Nobody believed that he didn't mean to set the fire."

"One of your kids set the house on fire?" Hunter didn't know why that surprised him.

"Joe gave up." Fortune ignored her partner. "We're going to make it, guys. Once we win the money, we're going to fix the house, and, who knows, we might even take a trip. Cowboy, help us out here. Where would you like to go?" she asked Hunter.

"To bed. My head is spinning. All you need to travel is some magic beans and a star to swing on."

"Magic beans—maybe you're right, cowboy. Let's find you a bed."

Hunter looked around. "Me, sleep here? Thanks but no thanks. They do lock those gates at night, don't they?"

"Yeah," Mickey said with a look of resignation on his face. "They sure do. But you can get out, dude."

"Then I guess it will be safe to leave you here. I'll pick you up in the morning, Fortune."

"What's the matter, don't you like the accommodations?" This question came from Jade, who hadn't taken her eyes from Hunter since he'd entered the house.

"I don't like jails. I like nice soft mattresses in rooms with windows that open if I want to let the world in—or," he added, lowering his voice, "if I want to get out."

"I see," Fortune said softly. But she wasn't certain that she did. The man had insisted on spending the night baby-sitting her, but once he'd seen the prison farm, he'd turned white as a sheet and backed away. Something about the place bothered him. "Not necessary, cowboy, we can meet at the starting point."

"No, I'll pick you up at the gate at eight-fifteen. We'll drive to the dealership together. I've arranged to leave my truck there."

"If you'd feel better about it, that suits me fine. See you in the morning."

Hunter turned and left the room, pausing in the doorway for one last look at the woman he'd be with for the next nine days. "Uh, Fortune," he said hesitantly, wanting to leave with some final comment that would settle his unease, "you do have shoes, don't you? Real shoes? It isn't safe to ride a bike without something substantial on your feet."

"I'll have something on my feet, Hunter. I promise." Though at the moment she wasn't certain what. Learning that Joe was gone explained what had happened to her tennis shoes, but she couldn't tell Hunter. Sports shoes were important to a kid, and a kid like Joe couldn't see the Hemingway cats barefoot. She understood that.

• • •

Hunter, on the other hand, was less understanding when she met him at the prison gate the next
morning wearing a pair of scuffed Keds and her
only other pair of clean jeans. There were no knees
in this pair either, and at the last minute she'd cut
them off, turning them into long shorts. Fortune
thought they went very well with the tank top she
wore, and they would certainly be cooler.

She had a rare headache, born of a sleepless
night trying to figure out what to do with her kids
while she was gone. There were too many runaways, and not enough guardian angels to provide
for them.

Tom and Rachel agreed to house them at the
farm until Fortune returned. There was plenty of
room. The Crisp County Prison Farm still produced its own food, so at least they could eat.

If the fire weren't enough, Lucy had disclosed
that, in spite of Tom and Rachel's influence,
the county had issued a citation for operating
a child-care center without a permit. Because
the fire had been set by a boy who'd been labeled
a juvenile delinquent, the entire program was
being threatened with closure. Now Joe had run
away.

Winning the scavenger hunt was her only hope.
Playing quirky word games and looking for a
needle in a haystack were two things Fortune had
always been able to do well. Her imagination had
soothed her loneliness and taken her everywhere a
child with nothing wanted to go. Books and dis-
carded magazines had fed the flames of Fortune's
imagination then, and necessity fed it now. Once

she and Hunter were given their clues, they'd find a way to win. They had to.

Hunter Kincaid was the closest thing Fortune had to a guardian angel, whether he knew it or not. He was her only hope. He'd drive that monster machine, and she'd navigate and decipher. She took a long look at the man getting out of the truck and sighed.

Her partner was wearing leather pants that looked like cowboy chaps over his jeans, and a vest over an army-drab T-shirt. He'd exchanged his Stetson for a baseball cap, but sunglasses still masked his eyes. Good, she thought. She didn't want to get lost in those blue eyes now. They had serious things to do, and she badly needed to stay in control.

"Morning, General Kincaid. Reporting for duty as ordered, sir," Fortune said, marching out through the gate, overlooking his frown at the same time she managed a jaunty salute.

Hunter took one look at her stretchy top and the shapely set of bare legs and groaned silently. His conclusion that his attraction to Fortune Dagosta was because of stress went right out the window. "This is your idea of proper scavenger-hunting attire?"

"It beats leather to hell and back. It was ninety-five degrees in the shade yesterday, or have you forgotten?"

"I remember. But suppose we have to go somewhere that's cold, not to mention the problem you're going to have with your bare skin after eight hours on a bike. You'll wish you were wearing leather to protect your body, wild woman."

"I didn't know that."

He pulled out one of the three cigars he'd allotted himself for the day and lit it. "Never mind, I figured this is about what I'd run into. I came prepared."

"Prepared for what? To die? You're dressed for war, and you're smoking cigars."

"I'm beginning to think that riding with you may become a war. As for my cigars, what's wrong with you, Ms. Dagosta? Are you some kind of health freak?"

"Maybe, but I have enough sense not to endanger my health by smoking."

"I knew it." He tapped the fire from his cigar and replaced the smelly object in his pocket. "And you probably don't eat steak either." Then he reached into the truck and pulled out a plastic bag.

As she started to answer, he held up his hand to stop her. "No—never mind. Forget I said that. I brought you some proper clothes."

Fortune gasped. "You did what? What's wrong with what I'm wearing?"

"Nothing, if you're going to the park or planning to weed the garden. But we don't know what is ahead of us, and I don't want anything to interfere with our winning this hunt. So take the clothes. You can pay me out of your part of the prize money."

Her part of the prize money? Fortune could have told him she was working on a way to convince him that she ought to have all the prize money. But she was afraid he might resist. For now, she needed to keep the man happy. For now, she needed him as much as he needed her. For now, she wouldn't think about the nine days she was about to spend with this man who'd already kept her awake half the night.

"How could you possibly know what size I wear?" She peered into the bag. For a moment she was so angry with his high-handed action that she could barely speak. Then she pulled out new jeans, a T-shirt, and a cap, and her fury quickly self-destructed.

It wasn't for her benefit, she told herself. He just wanted to make sure nothing interfered with their winning. She didn't need charity. They could win if she were nude. The clothes were an investment—not compassion. He was determined to win. She decided that had to be it, until she glanced at Hunter and caught the vanishing look of uncertainty on his face.

Hunter didn't want to admit that he was embarrassed over her pleasure. He fought back the color flushing his face with disdain. "I have a sister just about the same size as you, a fourteen-year-old sister. I thought these clothes would make the drive more comfortable for you. Sorry."

His sister. Fortune tried not to let him see that he'd caught her by surprise. Help was something she'd never asked for, and she didn't know how to accept it. She wouldn't admit it, but she couldn't remember how long it had been since she'd owned something that hadn't been worn before, or how long it had been since somebody had been concerned for her comfort.

Also in the bag were a blue chambray shirt, the same color blue as Hunter's eyes, and a pair of brand-new tennis shoes, just her size. Suddenly, she wasn't angry. She crumpled the bag and searched for some unemotional way to say thank you. She couldn't find one.

"You have a fourteen-year-old sister? Then I take it your mother *is* married," she finally said.

"Oh, yes," he answered, but the lightness returned to his voice. "Yes, she's married." He strode to the passenger side of the truck and opened the door, turning a questioning glare toward her. "Why would you ask that?"

"Because you seem so concerned about marriage, I figured you must have come from a broken home or had a bad relationship with a woman. Is this hang-up going to affect our partnership?"

"I assure you, the only relationship I'm concerned about is that of the number-fourteen team in the Panther Scavenger Hunt."

"Then we need to get along, don't we? So I thank you for the clothes, but let's get this straight, cowboy. Nobody put you in charge. We may be a team, but I'll decide what I wear, and what I don't."

Fortune didn't know why she was speaking so sharply. The man had just bought her a bag of new clothes. Maybe that was it. She'd been touched by his simple gesture, and she didn't want him to know how much. As always when something or somebody got too close, she shored up her defenses.

"Fine, you decide," he snapped back. "I just considered your well-being an investment in our future. If you want to take a chance on being uncomfortable, that's your choice—so long as it doesn't jeopardize our mission."

Fortune crinkled the bag as she closed it and stepped up into the trunk. She didn't want to spoil anything. She wanted their relationship to be good. But yuppie cowboys were people with whom she lacked experience. The only success she had was in dealing with runaways. And the only run-away in this truck was her heartbeat.

She slid her gaze across the seat as Hunter crawled in and slammed the door. Maybe that was her answer. Treat Hunter as if he were a runaway. There was something about him that was just as prickly. She leaned back and relaxed.

"Do we self-destruct in one minute?" she quipped.

"What?" Hunter turned around and started down the highway toward town.

"There was once an unlikely team, whose mis-sions were impossible dreams. They listened to the tape, deciphered their fate, and completed the preposterous schemes."

"And that's what you think this is—Mission Impossible?"

"No, cowboy, and I don't intend to let it become the Impossible Dream."

The director of the scavenger hunt repeated the information he'd given at the drawing, along with a new little piece of information. "There are several clues that are germane to all the teams," he said, "but the remainder of the clues are different. It was decided that having separate targets for each team would prevent collusion. All your clues have the same degree of difficulty and the same mileage differences between them."

A representative of the advertising agency han-dling the campaign added a second new piece of information: "There will be other little surprises along the way that we hope you'll enjoy. Any funds not used in the search are yours to keep."

The officials posed for pictures handing over the keys to the motorcycles, and the female team members were instructed to draw a list of clues from a glass bowl.

"Remember, today is Thursday. Your deadline is five o'clock next Friday. The team deciphering the greatest number of clues within this time frame wins. Good luck, guys and gals. You may open your envelopes."

"No," Hunter said, placing his hand over Fortune's. "Not here, not yet."

"But—"

"No matter what direction we go, we have to get to the intersection. Let's get there, away from the other teams, and then we'll study the clues carefully."

Disappointed, Fortune followed Hunter to the bike. He handed her a shiny black helmet and demonstrated the proper way to snap it closed. "Okay, let's hit it," he said, and threw one leg over the machine marked with the number 14. Fortune stared at the motorcycle nervously before she finally took a step closer.

"Get on, Fortune. Fifty-thousand dollars, remember?"

She did. Then she understood why she'd been so disturbed. It wasn't because of the machine. It was because of the man driving it—and the sudden knowledge that she was going to have to sit behind him, close behind him, for nine days.

Hunter, sensing her uncertainty, unsnapped his helmet and held out his hand. Slowly, Fortune took it, and he drew her up onto the bike. He explained where she was to put her feet, and how she should balance herself when they took a curve or came to a stop.

Then he pulled both her arms around his waist, pressing them firmly against his abdomen for a long minute. "Hang on tight, wild woman, we're on our way."

Three

Fortune didn't know whether she was flying or if she just felt as if she were. The hot air pushed aside by the bike was wrapping around her like a warm blanket, raising her body temperature even higher.

Hunter had worried for nothing. As long as she had the cowboy to hold on to, her skin didn't need protecting. If they had to travel anyplace cold, she'd be warm enough if she was stark naked.

Naked? There was something primeval about the picture that came unbidden into her mind; her and Hunter, without clothes, riding a big black stallion across a barren landscape. She felt a bead of perspiration roll down between her breasts, and she tried to lean back, away from the hard, muscular planes of his body.

At the intersection he pulled off the highway, followed a gravel drive behind a billboard, and came to a stop under a stand of loblolly pines. It was shady and cool beneath the trees, and except for the traffic on the interstate, it was quiet.

"Now, let's open the envelope and see what we have to work with," he said, flicking the bike's kickstand into place.

Fortune took the packet of information from its storage place and followed Hunter to a felled pine tree that made a good bench. Hunter's blond hair was tousled from wearing the helmet. It was damp from perspiration and curled wickedly across the base of his neck and his forehead. He looked like a little boy, a modern Huck Finn, on an adventure.

She was trembling slightly. It hadn't occurred to her before that she knew nothing about this man. She'd taken in every stray and homeless person who'd ever knocked on her door without a second thought. But this was different. She was becoming personally involved, and long ago she'd vowed not to let herself get close to a man. Friendship, but nothing more.

"What's wrong?" He sat on the log and waited, his thick lashes raising slowly as he met her gaze.

"Wrong? Uh, nothing. I was just thinking, I—we don't know much about—about each other, do we?" She tried to keep her expression bland, but she knew that she failed.

He was surprised at her uncertainty. Drafting a stranger to be his partner hadn't bothered him, because she'd been necessary to his plan. He was a man who set a steady course and didn't deviate. If there was a problem, he'd handle it. But Fortune's unexpected doubt could be a problem. Maybe a little reassurance on his part was in order.

"Okay, let's see. You know my name. My mother

lives in Greenville, South Carolina. Her husband is Hale Kincaid. He's on all the successful-people lists. I have a younger brother and sister who work in the family business, and the fourteen-year-old sister, who's still in school."

"Family business? Kincaid family business?"

To put some distance between them, Fortune walked away. She was standing beneath the billboard, the very large billboard advertising the Kincaid South, a hotel for the family, located just down the interstate. "You're part of Kincaid Hotels, Inc., and you're trying to win money in a contest?"

Hunter sighed. He'd been foolishly hoping to conceal his family's identity. To a woman who did her shopping at Goodwill, he no doubt appeared to be an ungrateful idiot. So much for any chance of simple understanding between them. Once again the Kincaid name threatened to brand him.

No, not this time, Hunter decided. Fortune Dagosta made up her own mind about people. He'd bet on it. And for some obscure reason it was important that she see him as "the cowboy" and like him for himself.

"Sorry, that's their business, only one of the Kincaid holdings—theirs, not mine. And yes, I do need this prize money," he said in a low voice. "So I guess you'll just have to trust me, Ms. Dagosta. I think that's little enough. After all, I trust you, and I picked you up at a prison farm."

She caught sight of a fleeting wry smile and realized that he was teasing her, trying to make her more comfortable. At the same time she knew that her acceptance of him was important. "You're right, " she admitted. "It's too late for either of us to back out."

"Well, open the envelope," he said roughly, erasing that moment of vulnerability. "I warn you that I'm not good at riddles."

"Don't worry, cowboy, I'm a whiz at solving puzzles, and I've covered most of this part of the country. So if we have to find something, I've probably seen it."

"Good," was all he said. He could have told her that he'd spent many years covering the Southeast, too, and the rest of the country as well. But while he would talk about his family if he was pushed, Hunter never talked about himself.

The envelope contained a single legal-size piece of paper. Fortune started to read to herself; then, breaking into a wide grin, she exclaimed, "Hunter, the clues—they're in rhymes."

"Rhymes? You mean like your limericks?"

"Yes, listen. This is the first one. 'Brown splattered red, midst Carolina hills of green. Dig out one of Frank's, let the sun shine through. And you will have solved an important clue.'"

Hunter shook his head. "Brown on red? Let the sun shine through? I don't understand."

"This is going to be hard," Fortune said, studying the paper. 'Dig something red out of something brown.' Dig. That could mean to understand, or it could literally mean to dig. Since this is a contest of movement, I don't think they're getting thoughty on us."

"What's red? Blood? 'Red out of brown' could be a blood bank. What do they think we are, vampires?"

Fortune sprang to her feet. "No. Rubies. Dig up

rubies. Out of Frank's mines. Franklin, North Carolina, has mines where amateurs can go and search for precious stones."

"North Carolina. Getting there's going to take a big chunk out of our week. Maybe we ought to try and figure the others out so that we can plan our route."

"Fine. Number two says, 'Mary Etta claims the queen, of chickens tall, with eyes that gleam. The Panther pres. would like a picture of you, beneath its beak—that's your second clue.'"

"I know that one," Hunter said with pleasure, "that's the statue of the Big Chicken in Marietta, Georgia, where they're famous for selling fried chicken."

Fortune cast a delighted smile on Hunter. Ever since she'd opened the package of clothes, her mental picture of him had changed. His attempt to reassure her by identifying himself when he'd clearly have preferred to keep his identity secret had only reinforced her instinct that she could trust him. They'd agreed that Hunter was to drive, she to navigate. That he was contributing to solving the puzzle was a plus neither had counted on. More than ever she was convinced that fate had intervened. They were going to win.

"North Carolina and North Georgia, what next?" Hunter was spreading maps across the tall dead summer grass.

"Number three—'Guarded by a frog for eons now, it has a mineral taste that soothes all care. Bring us a vial of Lithia gold, and we'll line your pockets with the kind you can hold.'"

"Lithia gold—nothing comes to mind. Here,

start checking." He stood up, pulled several travel guides from the storage area, and started looking through them.

"What do I look for?"

"Frogs, minerals, gold, I don't know."

But none of those clues showed up in their reference material, and Fortune had no idea what it meant. Finally, Hunter called a halt to the search. "Let's go on to the next clue. We'll come back to this one."

"In clue number four, 'North is South and West is East, and thousands look at the hideous beast. Bring us a tear from the creature's eyes, and Panther will reward you with a special prize.'"

"And the next one?" Hunter's forehead was creasing from worry.

"Number five. 'Green mounds of life and death lie lonely there. Man lived and died with loving care. Inside that darkness you'll see the light. Capture that beacon in the night.'"

"How many more?"

"Only two," Fortune said. "'There once was a man named Bobby, who made collecting bears his hobby. He has a little postman, he's the host with the most, man, go straight from Bobby to where?'

"Bobby—bears—Bobby Bear!" Fortune exclaimed excitedly.

"Who's Bobby Bear?"

"The country singer, in Nashville. Bobby Bear owns a shop where he sells nothing but bears. All we have to do is find a postman bear."

"Yeah," Hunter agreed, "and figure out how to get from Bobby to where."

"So I don't have all the answers." The truth was

slowly beginning to sink in. The first clues were easy. The other's weren't. Fortune felt the bitter taste of frustration in her mouth, and they hadn't even left Cordele yet.

"You say there's one more?"

"Yes, and it makes no sense. '"If you've gotten this far, it's time for some fun. You need a new hat, your hostess has one.' There are two tickets attached to the sheet. I don't know, Hunter, maybe this is a bad idea. How are we expected to solve these?"

"Maybe that's the point. Maybe they are just sending us in the right direction. We aren't supposed to figure out what we're going to find. Otherwise it would be too easy. The question is, do we go check out the chicken first, or go dig up some rubies?"

"The chicken first, I think," Fortune said slowly.

"It's in the same general direction as the ruby mines. Maybe we'll figure out something else along the way."

"Suppose we're wrong? We'll waste valuable time."

"Look. Everybody is in the same boat. They won't be able to solve them all either, and if they do, it won't be at the same pace. We'll just have to do our best."

"Damn! I didn't think it would be this difficult. The last scavenger hunt I went on sent us after an old green comb and a rooster's feather. This is hard."

He sounded disappointed. Before she thought, Fortune reached out and touched his arm. They were so close, she could feel the warmth of his body. "Don't worry, cowboy. You and me, it was fate. We're going to win."

In her blue-jean cutoffs, her stretchy top, and with those sun-kissed freckles, she looked like a pinup for *The Farmer's Almanac*. All she needed was a corncob pipe, and she'd make a perfect date for the Saturday night square dance. Why, then, was he fighting the impulse to take her in his arms? Hunter wondered.

"It won't be easy," he snapped.

"Why not?" she shot back, dropping her hand in her lap.

"Because nothing in my life ever has been."

"Never fear, Hunter Kincaid, you're with Fortune Dagosta now. I'm your lucky charm. The way I figure it, we ought to be at the chicken in time for an early dinner. I just love fried chicken, don't you?"

As he felt a faint stirring of unexpected camaraderie, he admitted, "Maybe," and started folding his maps. He didn't need directions to get to Marietta, that part of the state was one he knew well.

"Before we go, I want to give you a quick lesson in the operation of the Panther."

"Forget that," Fortune said, "I couldn't drive it even if you did. I'm not big on driving *cars*. At least I have a license for that."

"Maybe not, but you never know what could happen, and I believe in being prepared. Come here."

Fortune thought about the prize money and complied, though she knew with certainty that she'd never in a hundred years be able to drive the

LOVE AND A BLUE-EYED COWBOY • 51

Panther, even if it meant the difference between winning and losing.

"All right. This is the center stand. It keeps the back wheel off the ground so that we can't go anywhere. I'll sit behind you. Get on."

Fortune slid her leg over the big black machine. Hunter reached around her, taking her right hand in his and placing it on the handlebars. "This lever is the gas. Down here is the brake. On the left— put your left hand on this lever, Fortune. On the left is your clutch. Have you ever driven a car with a clutch?"

"Yes, at least I've done that."

"Well, it operates the same way, except you're dealing with levers instead of pedals."

Fortune concentrated on Hunter's instructions, not because she had any intention of driving the Panther, but because it was the only way she could still her racing pulse and keep her mind off the man's arms around her.

Finally, when he was satisfied that she at least understood the mechanics of the machine, he switched positions, offering one last warning: "Never, never get on the machine without your helmet."

Helmets fastened, they took off, flying along the interstate. One motorist after another, along with other bikers, slowed to examine the new Panther. Hunter knew that the contest was gaining national attention, but he hadn't realized how much.

Nor had he realized how aware he would be of the woman clutching him as if he were a life buoy and she were in danger of drowning. But he was. At least she was behind him. She couldn't know how disconcerting it was to feel her body pressed against his, her legs circling his bottom, her cheek against his neck.

Hunter soon decided that it was just as well that they couldn't talk on the bike. In spite of a little voice that said Fortune probably did manage to fumble through whatever came her way, his thoughts were a mass of confusion, and he didn't like being confused. He'd been through enough of that in his life, confusion of his own making. He didn't need a woman with freckles and heated fingertips to make things worse.

But that was just what he had.

He hadn't admitted even to himself how much he needed the money. There'd been too many years of moving from here to there, and one job to another, before he'd found himself racing a bike on the dirt tracks. His mother hadn't understood why he'd wanted to take such chances in a job that was dirty and low-paying. But he'd won and had built a reputation, his own reputation, about as far away from Kincaid Industries as he could get.

The accident had wiped him out, both physically and financially. When he'd repaid Hale, he'd had nothing left, neither a bank account nor a career. A man with fused vertebrae in his back couldn't race bikes, even if he wanted to.

They were heading up Highway 75, approaching Macon, when Fortune began nudging Hunter's shoulder. He inclined his head and leaned back, trying to hear what she was saying. She pressed closer, trying to explain. He might have understood her words if he hadn't been so conscious of her warm breath against his cheek. Finally, she motioned for him to pull over. He did.

"What's wrong? Are you one of those women who has to stop every hour when she's traveling?" His voice was rougher than he'd intended, but he felt out of control and didn't know how to cover his uncertainty.

"Don't be tacky, Tex," she said in mock dismay. "Look up there."

She was pointing to a billboard advertising the Ocmulgee Indian Mounds just outside of Macon. "'Green mounds of death'? Could this be what we're looking for?"

"That seems too easy," Hunter argued.

"Don't you think we'd better check it out?"

Hunter considered the question for a moment. If they were wrong, they'd lose valuable time. But if not, this sighting would be a gift. It was obvious that Fortune thought she was right. "Let's do it," he said.

A short time later they entered the Ocmulgee National Monument Park. At the visitors' center they picked up a brochure describing the Indian mounds and walked outside to study them.

"Okay," said Hunter, glancing around uneasily, "we're here, what now?"

Fortune studied the brochure. Maybe she'd been wrong in pushing Hunter to come there. She'd always made her way without worrying about what anybody thought. But now she was hesitant.

"Well, the clue said 'mounds of green for living and dying.' According to this, there are seven mounds: Cornfield, Funeral, McDougal, two temple mounds, and one simply called Southeast

Mound. Only one is open to the public. That's the Earth Lodge, which is a reconstruction of a ceremonial building, probably a temple or a meeting place."

"How do we know what we're looking for?"

"Some kind of light, a 'beacon in the night.' I don't know. I guess we'll just have to look around until we find it."

"Let's do it quick," he said, and started out at a marching pace.

"Hold on, cowboy. At the rate you're going, we could pass right by what we're searching for. I think this calls for a little meandering."

"Meandering?"

"Walking slow, Hunter, as if we're enjoying the park like two people on a spring day."

Something about his expression told Fortune that meandering was a speed with which Hunter was unfamiliar. But he obediently pulled up and began to study his surroundings.

The park was wearing May like a young woman in a green print frock. Flowering shrubs filled the air with sweet smells, and the sun shone brightly on the carpet of grass. They wandered along, not speaking, almost as if they really were on a date.

"Have you ever been here before, Hunter?"

"Nope. Unlike you, I always avoid federal facilities."

There it was again, his discomfort over being locked in. "The prison farm is a county, not a federal facility," she explained patiently, then realized that he was teasing again. She smiled.

"What does the pamphlet say anyway?" Hunter asked.

"It says the people who built these mounds were a tribe called the Mississippians. The Indians we know as the Creeks came later."

"What happened to them?"

"The Mississippians? Who knows. Probably outsiders arrived and brought every bad thing the white man ever had. Here it is, the Earth Lodge."

Inside the mound the temperature was cool. The facility was dimly lit, just as it might have been during its original use. Opposite the door was a clay platform shaped like a large bird.

Hunter walked to the center of the lodge. "Will you look at this. They must have held meetings here."

There were three seats on the platform and about fifty more on the bench around the wall. In the center was a fire pit.

"This is the first dark place we've been," Fortune commented, eyeing the indirect light coming from somewhere overhead. "I wonder what kind of light the Indians used inside."

A visitors' guide suddenly answered from behind them. She'd probably been there all along, and neither had noticed. "Before the mound was wired for electricity," she explained, "the Indians probably built a fire, or perhaps used some kind of primitive candles such as these." She indicated a woven basket beside the door that contained small branches wrapped with brush, like small torches.

"'Inside that darkness, you'll see the light.'" Fortune turned to Hunter and gave him an impulsive hug. "We've found it, cowboy, our 'beacon in the night.'"

"Can these be bought?" Hunter asked the guide.

"Not here, but I believe reproductions are being sold in the souvenir shop."

"You did it, wild woman." He responded to her hug by planting a kiss on her forehead. Fortune jerked away, pulling Hunter out the door and back down the path. Her heart was racing. They were a team. They'd solved the first clue. Hunter didn't let go of her hand until he had to pay for the torch at the visitors' station.

They stopped at a roadside ice-cream parlor for a quick lunch. Hunter had two footlong hot dogs. Fortune had one, to which she added chili and coleslaw. She ate quickly, then finished off Hunter's fries. She pocketed the extra packets of catsup and cleared off the table so that they could study the clues again.

By midafternoon they were standing beneath the fifty-six-foot chicken that appeared to be used as a directional marker for everybody in the Marietta, Georgia, area. It towered above the busy take-out restaurant like a hen sitting on her nest.

Hunter ordered a bucket of the good-smelling chicken with all the side dishes. Outside the building he talked a diner into taking their picture using the instant camera they'd been furnished by the hunt director.

When they went back to the bike, they saw a crowd of curious fans. "What's this, man?" one young man asked.

"It's a new Panther."

"Oh, yeah, you're on that scavenger hunt. Hey, there was another team just left here. I didn't get a chance to check out their machine up close. Man, this is a beauty."

Fortune felt her sense of euphoria evaporate. Somebody else had already been there. "Kincaid?"

"Stop it, we're not going to worry, wild woman. Just because they interpreted this clue doesn't mean they can solve all the others. We're going to stick to our plan."

He strapped the bag of food on the back, put her helmet on her head, and fastened it, running his fingertip lightly across her cheek. After a long moment he drew back and donned his helmet. "Let's find a place to eat and camp for the night."

"We're going to camp out?" Fortune slid into the seat behind him and moved forward until she could clasp her hands around him. She'd noticed that other women passengers seemed less concerned about holding on, but her confidence level hadn't quite reached that point yet. Now her fear of the machine fought a battle with her reluctance to be close to Hunter. At this point the battle was a draw.

"Yes, we're going to camp out, that was part of the rules. Remember? They even provided us with the necessary gear. That's what's in these rolls tied up behind your seat."

"But shouldn't we keep going?"

"Probably." He stretched and grimaced. "But if I'm going to last a week on this machine, I'm going to have to rest, at least until I get back in the swing of things."

"Oh, your back. I'm sorry. I'd forgotten all about it. I mean, I haven't forgotten, I was just thinking about other things. Oh, hell! . . ." Her voice trailed off. She couldn't even think of a limerick to get her out of the situation.

"Don't worry. I understand, and I know just the place to camp."

The place was a little spit of land that jutted out into Lake Lanier, the man made thirty-eight-thousand-acre storage lake used to generate electricity and supply water for the state of Georgia.

"Can we build a fire?"

"Not here, only in the campgrounds. So we'd better lay out our bedroll and get set for the night. Then we'll eat."

"Bedroll? Singular?"

"Bedrolls, wild woman, plural."

They unpacked their equipment and made their camp, bedrolls side by side. Hunter unstrapped his leather protective wear and pulled on a pair of shorts. They sat on the beach by the lake eating their chicken, biscuits, and beans, washed down with soft drinks Hunter had bought at the lakeside store.

Afterward Hunter retrieved his cigar and lit it, sending a thin trail of smoke into the air.

"Why do you smoke, cowboy?"

"Same reason you eat so fast and hoard food, wild woman—it gives me a sense of security."

"Smoking gives you security? How?"

"My father smoked. I remember sitting with him on the porch, smelling his cigar, and I knew things were all right."

"How old were you?"

"I don't know, about five or six."

In the water a fish jumped, breaking the surface

with a whack that sent quick little waves slapping the earth at the water's edge. Then the lake settled back down to a gentle undulation. A fat buttery moon rose over the water in the distance, lighting the area so that Fortune and Hunter could see each other without a fire.

Fortune would have liked to ask more, but she didn't. Hunter would just clam up, and she wouldn't learn anything else. When he was ready, he'd tell her—just as Mickey and Joe had.

"This is peaceful, isn't it?" she said softly.

"Yes."

But Hunter's voice wasn't relaxed. He shifted often, changing his position and stretching his legs. Fortune knew that he was in pain.

"What happened to your back, cowboy?"

"An accident."

"What kind of accident? No, don't tell me. It happened on a motorcycle?"

"Yes, but don't panic. Normally, I'm a very careful street driver. I was on a racetrack, in the lead, when I crashed. My bike wanted to go straight, and I didn't."

Fortune turned toward Hunter. "You were racing, on a motorcycle?"

"That's what I do, or rather what the Bounty Hunter did."

"You were badly hurt, weren't you?"

"Let's just say that my spine isn't laid out like it was before the doctors got hold of me."

"Doctors? You've had surgery? When?"

"Twelve weeks ago."

"Hellfire, cowboy. And you're out here riding that—that thing?"

"Yep."

Fortune wanted to rail at him about taking care of himself. She wanted to tell him to go home and take it easy, but she couldn't. The man was a daredevil. She'd tried to ignore his reason for entering the contest, charging it off to a lark, but nobody was that much of a fool. Nobody chose to hurt, not without good reason.

"Didn't they give you something to take?"

"Oh, yeah, liniment and pain pills. But the pills make me too sleepy to drive."

Back surgery. Liniment. Massage. Fortune began to smile. One of her many temporary jobs had been as a masseuse. She'd been trained by one of the best. Hunter didn't know it yet, but he'd hit the jackpot.

"Did you bring your prescriptions with you?"

"Yes. I'll probably take a pain pill before I go to sleep." He tossed the stump of a cigar into the lake. "At least part of my instructions fit right in with camping out. I'm supposed to sleep on a hard surface."

"Not yet, cowboy. Before you go to sleep, I have a little something for you." She got up and stood over him.

Hunter glanced at her suspiciously. "What?"

"First, take off your clothes." She turned toward the bike, ignoring Hunter's gasp as she began to paw through the section of the storage area where his things were packed. The first container was shaving cream. The second container was an aspirin-based lotion, liniment.

Take off his clothes? He'd known she was a flake. It shouldn't have come as a surprise to him—but it did. It took Hunter a moment to find his voice. "What are you doing, wild woman?"

"Something I excel in, cowboy, something that is going to make you feel very good. I promise. Why are you still dressed?"

"Fortune, I don't think that it would be a good idea for us to—I mean, we're going to be together for seven more days, but as you said, we don't really know each other."

Hunter knew that he was fumbling badly, but he'd been surprised. He'd never had a woman direct him to take off his clothes, not without some kind of foreplay or hint of her interest.

Fortune began to grin. The cowboy thought she wanted his body. Well, that might not be an unpleasant idea under normal circumstances, but he was right in his refusal. Making love to her partner would definitely be a bad move. Her mind agreed, though her hormones seemed ready to debate the issue.

"Relax, cowboy. This is not what you think. I'm going to give you a body massage."

He still didn't believe her.

"I'm serious. I spent six months once working with a master masseuse. I never got a license, but I can do wonderful things to your body with my hands. Take off your shirt and turn over on your stomach."

"Why would you want to do that? I mean, why the massage?"

"Because you're in pain and I can help."

Hunter simply stared at her.

Fortune wasn't sure he'd give in. But physical discomfort eventually won out over his resistance to taking orders. That he pull his T-shirt over his head was proof enough of the degree of his pain.

Fortune sat back on her heels studying his strong body until he was ready.

Uncapping the liquid, she moved over to his bedroll and knelt beside him. She poured a dollop of the liniment still warm from the sun, into her palm and began with the muscles in Hunter's neck.

He was tense, very tense, and Fortune had to work slowly at first. With firm motions she kneaded out the knots of tension and resistance. Without speaking, she performed her magic, refilling her palm with liniment and working out across his shoulders and down each arm. His fingers came next before she moved back to the massive muscles that bunched in his shoulders. Carefully, with a lighter touch, she gave her attention to his backbone, following the lines of the surgery scars, watching for a wince or other reaction that told her she was causing him pain.

None came. Instead a kind of warmth began to steal across his body, radiating out from her fingertips like those waves from the disturbance in the lake's surface. Little by little she worked down his back, along the waistline of his shorts and white knit briefs, sliding her fingers in a downward motion beneath the band. She felt him stiffen suddenly.

"Did I hurt you?"

"No, it isn't that." There was an intimacy about her movements, an intimacy he didn't welcome yet couldn't quite bring himself to end.

"Then what?" Her hands were resting on the lower part of his back.

His body began to undergo a subtle change that

overrode his casual, "Nothing, Fortune. Aren't you about done?"

"Almost," she said as she pulled away and began applying her magic touch to his feet, moving slowly up his well-corded calves, past his knees to the muscles now twitching in his thighs.

Hunter didn't speak. He was long past the point of relaxation. What she was building now was a new kind of tension, and he didn't know how much he could take.

"Turn over," she said, and leaned back on her heels.

"Not in this lifetime, wild woman."

"Why? What's wrong?"

"Just what kind of master did you learn from?"

"She worked with a group of chiropractors, why?"

"You'd be a smash down at Sadie's Special Parlor. I'll bet those chiropractors did a booming business."

"Oh." Now she understood why he didn't want to turn over. Suddenly, the good feelings began to evaporate. She recapped the liniment, stood, and made her way to the bike, where she stored the medication.

At that moment a bullfrog's baroque call echoed through the night.

Fortune brushed off her feet and sat on her sleeping bag. "I wish I had a light. I'd like to study those clues a little more."

For a long time Hunter didn't speak. "Tomorrow will be soon enough, Fortune," he finally said. "We'll get a good night's sleep, and come morning, we'll be on our way. With any luck we'll stumble across another answer or two."

"Fine," Fortune agreed, and slid down into the bag. She lay listening to the sounds of the night, thinking about the day and how pleasant it had been. She hadn't expected it to be.

Her partner was so cynical, so determined to be cool. He seemed to separate himself from everybody, even his family. She remembered his reference to his father as his mother's husband. Yet every now and then his dry sense of humor slipped out, and when it happened, he quickly retreated behind his laid-back, uninterested manner.

In the darkness Hunter's body throbbed insistently. Everything about him rejected being close to someone. Yet he couldn't control his response to his partner. He knew there was nothing sexual intended in the massage. She simply helped everyone who needed help.

No, she didn't simply help, she helped with blind determination. She was such a little thing, yet there was nothing small about her heart or her plans. She'd expected to win the contest and use the money to repair the roof on the house where her motley group of children hung out.

Children. He couldn't get over the way she'd hugged Mickey, comforted the tall, gangly boy who was worried about his friend. She'd done the same for him, expressing her compassion first by touching his arm, then with the hug, and finally with her fingertips.

"Fortune?"

"Yes."

"Thanks for the rubdown. I really needed it. I'm sorry I said what I did about Sadie's."

"That's okay. I never worked in one of those kinds of parlors, but who knows, under different circumstances I might have. Can I get you something for the pain?"

"No, I'll be fine now."

He knew full well that the only pain she could treat was a pain he refused to acknowledge. He had to force himself to look at their journey one day at a time. He'd got through the first one. He had seven more to go.

Hunter closed his eyes and tried to relax. It wasn't the days that he was worried about, it was the nights.

Four

The drive to Franklin, North Carolina, was incredibly beautiful. After a quick cup of early morning take-out coffee, Fortune and Hunter were more than ready for a lunch of country ham and spiced apples at the hundred-year-old Whittier Mill Inn. They ate on an open porch built out over the river that turned the mill to grind the corn.

"Do you always eat so heartily?" Hunter asked with amusement.

Fortune paused in her chewing and reflected on his question. "I suppose I do. And I eat much too fast. I guess it's a holdover from my childhood."

"Why, were you afraid somebody was going to take it away from you?"

"Yes."

Hunter was only joking until he saw the stricken look his words caused. "Sorry, I didn't mean anything, wild woman."

"Why do you keep calling me that? I'm not wild. At least I don't consider myself wild—unless you try to hurt someone I care about. Then I'm likely to turn into one of those panthers our motorcycle is named for."

This morning she wasn't wearing any makeup. Her freckles were tinted the pale pink of someone who'd spent time in the sun. Her cheeks were pink as well, made so by the hot wind as they rode. She had a wide-eyed innocent look about her. But the pressure of her breasts against his back as they rode definitely belied the image of her as a young girl.

Still dressed in her cutoffs, she'd exchanged the tank top for the olive-drab T-shirt he'd bought. That was a mistake. At least the tank top had some kind of stretchy stitching that allowed it to expand. The T-shirt was plain, formfitting, and clung to her small breasts. Fortune looked like anything but a fourteen-year-old child. Today her hair had lost its stiff peaks. Now it was merely short, windblown, and charming.

"I suppose I call you 'wild woman' for the same reason you call me 'cowboy.' It was the first impression I had of you, dancing around on one foot and spitting mad. Does it offend you?"

"No," she answered, and realized she meant it.

Two kinds of people had nicknames. There were the Vicky, Sherry, and Barbie people, important to the person giving the nickname. Then there were the insider names allotted to people so totally irksome that the name was always cruel or unpleasant. She didn't need to call those to mind—she'd heard them often enough as a child.

While "wild woman" wasn't an endearing nickname, it wasn't unpleasant. In fact, it appealed to her in a way she couldn't explain. She smiled.

"Does it bother you for me to call you 'cowboy'?"

He considered her question. "Not at all. I guess it's the first personal nickname I've ever had that wasn't a put-down."

"You mean other than Bounty Hunter?"

"That's different. That's business, or it was. I guess those outlaws riding the circuit are glad the Bounty Hunter got shot down at the pass. Are you about finished eating?"

He stood. Fortune allowed him to hurry her. She had the feeling he'd revealed something about himself that he'd like to take back. It couldn't be the reference to being a bounty hunter. That was business. The only thing left was the personal reference, the reference to a put-down.

Hunter Kincaid wouldn't take being put down easily, and she'd already figured out that he didn't get close enough to people to have any kind of personal relationship at all, certainly not nicknames.

"Okay, cowboy, I think we ought to plan where we're going next, assuming that the Franklin mines clue pans out."

"Pans out?" He paused. "Puns and limericks, but no sculleries. Shall we get to it, partner?"

There it was again. That droll humor and the quick, half-hidden smile that disappeared as quickly as it came.

"Good idea," she agreed, and followed him to the gazebo outside the inn where they could sit undisturbed in the sun. "Bobby Bear, we know. That's in Nashville. I've been thinking the new hat clue might suggest Minnie Pearl. You know, the country-music comedienne who always wears the hat with the price tag."

"I know. We could head for Nashville from here."

"It's the others I'm stumped on. I've been thinking about the Lithia gold and the crying creature. Nothing rings a bell. Maybe we ought to buy some more travel guides, the kind that tell you places to see and how to get there."

Hunter swore. He should have thought of that. If he hadn't been so tied up with his new partner, he would have. "Great," he snapped, "now you think of deluxe travel guides, when we're out in the middle of nowhere."

"I'm guessing there'll be a local bookstore in Franklin. Sometimes the owners are historians and stock the kind of thing we're looking for; if not, at least they'll have tourist information."

"Uh-oh. If I'm not mistaken, one of our competitors just drove by."

"Oh, no! We'd better go."

"Yeah." Hunter stood, then stopped and stretched, pressing his lower back with his hand, as if he were mashing out the kinks.

"How's the back doing?" she asked, suddenly remembering her hands had been in that same spot the night before. She'd successfully avoided thinking about the massage she'd given Hunter in the dark by the lake. She didn't want to remember the results of her attempts to relieve his tension. But saying it and doing it were two different things.

The tension between them was still there and getting stronger. Hunter knew it as well as she. He swallowed hard and started back to the parking area. His body stance answered her question better than words could have.

At the visitors' station outside Franklin they ran

into their first real decision: which mine to visit. There were several in the area.

"Read the clue again, Fortune."

"'Dig out one of Frank's, let the sun shine through. And you will have solved an important clue.' It doesn't specify any particular mine, Kincaid, just that we find a 'red one.' So, pick whatever sounds good."

Hunter studied the list and the map. There were several mines on Allen Road. He didn't suppose it mattered which one they chose.

Six miles down the highway the signs directed him to either Youkon Mine or Caler Creek Mine. Youkon struck him as too commercial, and he passed it by, turning instead at the less pretentious Caler Creek sign.

Past the rail fence, topping the hill, he came to a stop in the parking area opposite a long trough with a shed over it. People were busily working what looked like screens back and forth.

"This is it?" Fortune questioned. "Where's the mine?"

"Let's ask." Hunter unwound his long legs and reached back to assist Fortune.

The lady at the entrance building identified herself as Zeena and collected the entrance fee. She explained that the dirt was pre-dug, from the site, and transported to the shed for easy mining. "Three buckets for one dollar," she said, "and you can stay the whole day."

"How will we know if we have a ruby?" Hunter asked.

"My husband's out there. He'll tell you."

"If we hold the ruby up to the light, can we see the sun through it?"

The woman cut her eyes toward the parking lot and then back to Hunter and Fortune. She began to smile. "You two on that scavenger hunt?"

"Yes, we are. How'd you know?" Fortune's distrust showed in her voice.

"It's all over the news. Heard about it last night. Yes. If you hold the stone up to the light, you can see through it."

Hunter paid for three buckets' worth of dirt and carried them, inside, or outside, as it turned out to be. For a moment he studied the other miners who were sifting their dirt through the fine-netted object that he'd have called a strainer, and washing it away with the water that was being pumped through the sluice, leaving only the small rocks and stones behind. In no time they'd unearthed not one but three stones that the mine owner declared to be rubies. Fortune held them up to the light and verified that the sun shone through. On their way out the woman named Zeena called them over to the counter and handed them an envelope.

"They told me to give you this envelope when you left."

Fortune looked at Hunter. "Envelope?"

Hunter slid his sunglasses from the top of his head back down to the bridge of his nose. "Ah, yes. They did warn us that there'd be surprises. Looks like we've just gotten our first one." He led the way over to a picnic table beneath the trees. "Okay, open it."

Inside there was a slip of paper.

"'Catch the Chattanooga Choo-Choo. They have a room for you. Get your tickets stamped, and there's an extra prize too.'"

Both she and Hunter understood that clue. They

were being directed to the old Southern Railway Terminal Station in Chattanooga. Enterprising businessmen had transformed the terminal into the finest array of restaurants in the city. Private rail cars had been transformed into sleepers, and the baggage-storage areas into little shops. A modern full-service hotel had been built adjacent to the railroad lines for those guests who preferred more modern conveniences.

"Well, that settles that. We're on our way to Chattanooga," Fortune said, folding the paper and replacing it in the envelope.

"Not necessarily. Maybe they're trying to divert us. Claiming an extra prize could cost us the big one."

"Could be," Fortune agreed.

Hunter retrieved his road map and began studying it. "On the other hand we have to spend the night somewhere, and Chattanooga is between us and Nashville. You call it, wild woman, shall we stop off at the Choo-Choo?"

"A *room*?" Fortune questioned. "As in take a real bath and sleep in a real bed? Oops, I forgot. Sorry, cowboy, you can always sleep on the floor."

Fortune wiped the perspiration from her upper lip. She added the rubies to the envelope with the bonus clue and thought about their situation. Hunter had gamely carried on, but she knew that his back had to be bothering him. A hot soak in the tub followed by another massage was probably a good idea.

"A floor with a carpet sounds good to me right now."

"Then I say, let's go for it. Unless," she amended, "we run into something else along the way."

"Like what?"

"I don't know, but it seems that these first clues have been almost too easy to solve. We have too much time left. Maybe we're going to discover lots of little diversions along the way."

Hunter had been thinking the same thing. Though neither of them had any idea about the Lithia gold, or the creature, the other clues were like following the Yellow Brick Road. Sooner or later he was sure they'd hit a real zinger. Maybe a comfortable night's sleep was wise.

"Okay, wild woman. Let's get out of here."

As they were leaving the Caler Creek Mine, a second Panther pulled up, and the man and woman slid off and hurried inside, ignoring Fortune and Hunter in their haste.

"Looks as if we got here first this time, but not by much," observed Hunter, glancing at his watch. "I think we'll hunt out a bookstore here in Franklin. We need to do some research."

They headed back to town, stopping at a service station where Hunter used some of their traveling money to fill the motorcycle's tank.

"The station operator says there's a bookstore in a shopping center not too far away," he said as he cranked the engine and pulled back onto the highway.

The store manager was very helpful in providing tourist guides published by the various oil companies. They highlighted everything in the southeastern area, with a list and directions to nearby restaurants and hotels.

Fortune put aside her normal inclination to tear into the books immediately and followed Hunter's suggestion that they wait until they reached Chattanooga to study them.

"Suppose what we're looking for is between here and Chattanooga?" Fortune asked.

"Then we'll see it, just the way you spotted the Indian mounds. Keep a sharp eye, wild woman."

She did. But nothing presented itself, nothing but a more intimate acquaintance with Hunter's back and powerful thighs. Even the touch of pink mountain laurel and crab-apple blossoms that were beginning to burst into bloom didn't divert her attention. And she badly needed diverting.

If she'd been standing, she would have said her knees were wobbling. From the position she was occupying, she had to call it more of a jiggle, a jiggle that began in the pit of her stomach and radiated downward to the tips of her newly encased toes.

"Something wrong?" Hunter called over his shoulder.

"No!" She had to lean forward, pressing her cheek against his shoulder, to be heard.

"Then why are you manhandling my body?"

Hellfire, her elbows were dug into his sides, and her fingertips were underneath his T-shirt, finger-painting his chest, and she didn't know how they'd got there. "Sorry!" she yelled, moved her hands, and got rocked back by the air pressure whipping around Hunter's body. "Whoa!"

Hunter pulled over to the side of the road and brought the cycle to a stop. He lifted his leg across the handlebars and turned to face Fortune.

"Look, wild woman. We're going to have to get past this sex thing, or we're heading for trouble."

"Sex thing? How dare you? I'm not interested in you or your body, cowboy."

"Oh, no?" His gaze drifted down her face, then her neck, and came to a pause on her breasts.

She watched her nipples turn into tight buds under the soft fabric of her shirt.

"Let's not lie to each other, Fortune. You're one lush lady, and I'm having just as much trouble with this partnership as you are. What do you think we ought to do about it?"

Fortune crossed her arms over her chest and let out a long breath. "I think that we'd better get moving, Kincaid. I'll take care of my problems, and you take care of yours."

"Oh?" His eyebrows lifted.

"That's not what I meant. What I meant was— Oh, hell. I don't know what I meant. There was a woman from . . ." But this time she couldn't make a rhyme. Hunter had a way of stealing her words as well as her thoughts. She couldn't even think of a limerick.

"We're already in trouble, aren't we, wild woman?"

"I'm afraid so."

She was practically melting against him, on the side of a public highway, in the midafternoon sun. The smell of laurel wafted through the air. The earth was bright and new and green. Fortune took another deep breath.

"Hunter, I think you'd better drive this motorcycle to Chattanooga. Whatever is happening between us has to stop. We have miles to go before we can—"

"You're right," he agreed. "Get your feet up, wild woman. I don't want to destroy those new shoes."

He whirled around, restarted the motor, and drove away.

"What about my feet?" she yelled.

"If I injure your feet, you'll just have to stay in bed."

But the wind caught his words and flung them away. All Fortune heard was that she'd have to stay somewhere. "Stay where?"

In my bed was the answer he didn't give, the answer that came vividly to life as he felt her settle back into the neat little package she made behind him. He felt like one of the Teenage Mutant Ninja Turtles, wearing Fortune Dagosta like a shell.

Everybody knew that a turtle depended on its shell for warmth and protection. Fortune laid her cheek against Hunter's back and tightened her grip. He didn't know about the protection bit, but he was beginning to wish that the scavenger hunt had been held in December. He was much too warm, and he never asked for protection.

Maybe the Chattanooga Choo-Choo was air-conditioned. Surely, the scavenger-hunt people had reserved two separate rooms.

He was wrong.

The reservation manager at the Chattanooga Choo-Choo was expecting them, though not by name. Hunter and Fortune's reservation was for a private parlor car.

The bell captain escorted them to their car, demonstrated the vending machine complete with sodas, beer, and snacks, the sofa that could be made into a bed if they'd had children.

"Wow! This motorcycle company believes in going first class, don't they?" Fortune plopped down on the velvet-covered king-size bed and leaned back. She'd seen the king-size bed and panicked, until the hotel employee had demonstrated the sofa.

Relax, Fortune, she told herself. They were just two people sharing a room. She'd done that for most of her life, often with people she'd known a lot less about. The line of thought was meant to reassure her. It didn't. Hunter wasn't a stranger, no matter how much she pretended he was. And that was the problem.

They'd acknowledged the S-word, and the letter seemed to be branded on Fortune's body. She could feel it throbbing. Hunter was standing at the doors, closing it behind the bellboy. Fortune was still stretched out on the bed.

"The first thing I'm going to do," she said brightly, "is take a bath. What about you?"

"I think I'll just sit here and unwind while I look through these travel books."

Fortune didn't miss the strain in his voice. She realized what she'd just said and winced. Staying in the hotel was for Hunter's benefit. "Sorry, cowboy. I didn't think. You take a bath first. Fill that tub up and take a long, hot soak."

"That's all right, you go first."

"No, you. You're the one with the bad back."

"Take a damned shower, Fortune! I can wait."

They were practically screaming at each other. Fortune opened her mouth to protest, but the undeniable flame of heat scissored down her legs again. He was right. She'd take a quick shower, and then he could stay in the tub as long as he liked. She grabbed her pack and scurried into the bathroom, turning on the shower as she pulled out the new clothes Hunter had bought for her. Quickly, she soaped up, shampooed her hair, and rinsed off. Hunter was still standing by the door when she came out, drying her hair as she tried not to look at him.

She could tell he was tired. His face was drawn, but, even now, without the sunglasses, his blue eyes seemed to challenge her. His eyes, without the words to accompany them, spoke of rumpled sheets and the invitations not yet acknowledged. Sexual tension arched from him, catching her in its force, and again her feet seemed welded to the floor.

"Your turn, cowboy."

He nodded, moved past her into the steamy bathroom, and turned on the hot water in the tub. As it filled, he pulled clean jeans and a shirt from his pack.

Fortune turned on the reading light by the chair and opened the travel book. She heard Hunter slide into the tub, and forcing her attention to her book, she began to read.

The index listed Lithia Springs, Georgia. She turned to the page and scanned for the description. "Bingo! Hunter, I found it, the mineral springs in Lithia Springs, Georgia. And there's a frog, a thousand-year-old frog rock on the premises."

"Good, anything on the creature?"

"Nope, nothing yet. That's the only clue without a single word to direct you. 'North is South and West is East . . . Bring us a tear from the creature's . . . eyes.'"

Running her fingers through her hair, she dried it quickly. She finished one book and was almost

done with the other when she realized that Hunter had been soaking for a long time. Carefully, she marked her place in the book and stood up. The door to the bathroom wasn't completely closed. A sliver of light shone through the opening. Fortune tried to see inside, but the angle didn't allow her any view of him.

"Hunter?"

There was no answer.

"Hunter?" she called again. Still no answer.

Fortune pushed open the door and rushed in. "Hunter!"

At the same time he bobbled his head, blinked his eyes, and stood straight up.

"What's wrong?"

Fortune could only stare in disbelief. Wrong? Nothing. Not one solitary thing that she could see, and she could see it all.

"Fortune, I don't really mind being gawked at, but I'm not used to having it done while I'm not at my best."

"That's all right," she whispered, backing slowly out of the room. "I'm a secondhand person, you know, and I can honestly say that Goodwill would love to get a chance at you."

Dinner was a strained affair at first. Neither Fortune nor Hunter could get past the great bathroom encounter. Fortune couldn't get the scene out of her mind. She felt as if she were watching some Technicolor movie, with the film stuck on one frame.

They chose a table on the Palm Terrace overlooking the great fountain beyond the floor-to-ceiling glass windows. The menu included a choice of meals, and both settled on the special New Orleans shrimp. Meanwhile, knowing his partner's appetite, Hunter ordered a selection of appetizers that included special muffins and breads.

Fortune immediately dived in. By the time their shrimp arrived, she'd made a huge dent in the appetizers, and they'd got past the awkward moment and were able to talk.

"Tell me about your children," Hunter asked. "How'd they get to be yours?"

"We just seemed to find each other. Lucy and I met in Atlanta. We were both on the road, so to speak."

"You mean you were hitchhiking?"

"Not exactly. Lucy was on her way home, and her car got as far as Atlanta and quit. I was on a temporary job at Jake's Coffee Shop when she came in. A week later we were both on our way to her family home in South Georgia.

"The one with no roof."

"Yep, only it had a roof then, and it had Mickey."

"Mickey?"

"He was sleeping in the barn. Jade came the next week. Somebody she met along the way had told her about the barn and Lucy's aunt, who was always good for a meal. Mickey found Beau hitchhiking on the freeway about a month later."

"What about Joe?" Hunter was curious about the boy who'd burned the roof and entered Fortune in the contest to win money for repairs.

"A friend brought Joe to us. He caught him foraging in the trash behind the local café."

"Didn't you catch any flak from the authorities?"

"Yes and no. There isn't a shelter for juveniles in

the county. It's a matter of shipping them to one of the state facilities. When you're dealing with runaways, the officials are more than willing for somebody to offer them a place to stay. Rachel and Tom were working with us to make our shelter a permanent facility."

Hunter saw Fortune's restraint fall away as she talked about her children. The children had been alone and needed a place to stay. Lucy had inherited a house with plenty of rooms.

Dressed in the new blue chambray shirt and a pair of regular jeans, Fortune Dagosta was charming. She'd touched her lips with pale pink lipstick that brought out the color in her cheeks. Her hair was bouncy, swinging from side to side as she talked. She had energetic hair, he decided, which matched the rest of her very well.

"Something wrong, cowboy?"

He'd been staring at her. If she'd asked a question earlier, he hadn't heard it. He had to replay the last few minutes in his mind to pick up the conversation. They'd been talking about the runaways that Fortune had taken in.

"But what about Lucy, didn't she mind? Didn't her family mind?"

"That's why she was going home. Her aunt had been living in the house, and when she died, she left the house to Lucy. Heck, you saw it. It was practically a mansion. Neither one of us had ever had a real house before, not since—" She broke off. "What about you, where do you live?" She helped herself to the last shrimp and deftly changed the subject.

"I already told you my mother lives in Greenville, South Carolina."

"And your sisters and brother?"

"My brother, Robert, is only sixteen. He lives at home, like my youngest sister, Penny, and works in one of the hotels part time. My sister Julie is twenty-three. She's the assistant to the president of Kincaid Chemical Corporation."

"And the president is . . . " Fortune prompted, knowing that Hunter had talked all around his father without mentioning him.

"My mother's husband."

"Come on, cowboy. If his name is Kincaid and your name is Kincaid and he's married to your mother, he must be your father—even a wild woman like me can figure that out."

"No, he's not my father. My father died when I was eight years old, working in the Kincaid Chemical Company plant." Hunter laid his napkin on the table. "Are you about finished here?"

"I am not, and neither are you. Since we don't have to pay for it, I intend to have one of those sinfully delicious desserts before I go anywhere."

"You've already eaten all the bread and a full shrimp dinner complete with baked potato. And you want dessert too?"

"I do, and I want an answer to my question. Is Mr. Kincaid your father or not?"

"He adopted me when he married my mother. It wasn't my idea, and I fought it until I realized how much it hurt my mother. I had to become Hunter Kincaid, but I didn't have to like it. There was just so much compromise I could handle. At sixteen I moved out."

Fortune gave a little gasp. "I haven't seen it, but somehow I don't think the house you moved out of was anything like the one Mickey and the rest of us ran away from."

"No, I guess not. But I've gotten along all right without fine furniture and servants."

"Sure, I never could take having somebody wait on me either," Fortune said airily. "I lived with my grandmother, after my mother died. She used to say, 'Waste not, want not.' And boy, she never wanted for anything. Me? I learned a lot about want. But that's another story."

"You lived with your grandmother? What happened to your folks?"

"My mother died when I was six years old."

"Your father?"

"Died last year. At least he was buried last year. He died a long time ago."

She didn't have to say any more about the man who'd deserted her for most of her life; her tone of voice said it for her. She stared at the table as the waiter removed their plates and took their orders for pecan pie with ice cream. She took one look at Hunter's face and knew that the man he called Hale, instead of father, was a subject for another night.

Most of the other diners were gone when they finished their pie. Fortune swiped the last two packets of crackers and stuffed them in her pocket. The waiter poured their after-dinner coffee and left.

Hunter was still very quiet. Fortune covered his hand with her own. "Looks like you were right, cowboy, we're a pair. Two misfits out of somebody's bad dream."

"I'll take the couch," Hunter said as he followed Fortune into the sleeping car.

"That's dumb. You're two feet taller than I am. The couch fits me. You take the bed."

Hunter locked the door and turned off the light over it. "We could share it," he suggested. "I think it may be part of the rules."

"I don't think so. They probably assumed that two people making up a team are either married or—very close. But then there's the matter of two bedrolls and the sofa bed. I think they covered all the possibilities."

"You want to take the bathroom first?"

"Uh, no, you go ahead."

"Whatever you say, but I have to tell you, wild woman, that I don't sleep in pajamas when I'm camping, and when I sleep in a bed, I don't wear anything at all. So if you want to get into your nightie while I'm brushing my teeth, I'll give you time."

"Hunter, I don't sleep in a nightie."

"Oh."

Fortune pulled out the sofa and began making it up. Hunter watched for a minute, then went into the bathroom and made a great show of running water, flushing the toilet and brushing his teeth.

Fortune smiled. She wouldn't have thought so, but he was more nervous than she was.

She peeled off the new jeans and shirt, pulled a tank top over her head, crawled into her bed, and pulled up the sheet. She was nervous.

When the bathroom door opened, she pretended to be asleep. Through half-closed eyes she watched as Hunter leaned forward in a series of aerobic stretching exercises before sliding his briefs down his muscular legs and climbing into bed. He switched out the light.

When she was certain that he was asleep, Fortune slid from her bed and into the bathroom, where she rinsed out her T-shirt and panties. Hanging them on the edge of the tub, she turned out the light and went back into the bedroom.

"Good night, wild woman," Hunter said softly. "If you change your mind about the bed before morning, feel free to join me."

Fortune didn't answer. Changing her mind wasn't the issue. She'd wanted to share his bed since she'd startled him awake in the tub. Fortune never had been one for planning. And the last thing she'd thought about when she'd left Cordele was making love to her partner. Turning on her side, Fortune admitted that while she might take some foolish risks to help a child, she'd never been quite so tempted to take the kind of risk that would create an unwanted one.

She'd stay where she was.

But she couldn't keep from thinking about the cowboy with the intense blue eyes. He was so close and yet so far away.

Five

The little refrigerator that had been filled with snacks and sodas the previous night was empty when Fortune opened it the next morning. So was the parlor car. So was the king-size bed. She had the odd feeling that the previous day and night had all been a dream. Now she'd woken up to the truth.

Until she went into the bathroom.

Her lace panties and T-shirt had been moved from the side of the tub. They'd been laid carefully across the towel rack.

Beads of water still hung on the tiled shower wall, and a rumpled towel lay across the edge of the tub. Hunter had taken a shower. He'd probably walked around in his briefs, and she'd slept through it.

Fortune's face burned with the thought of his discovering her lacy underwear. She'd intended to wake first and put her laundry away.

"Fortune? Are you dressed?"

Hunter's footsteps sounded in the parlor car.

"Yes," she said quickly, stuffing the panties under her tank top, "but I'm starving. What happened to the snacks?"

"Oh, I knew you'd want to take them, so I went out and got a small cooler. They're already packed. They don't have tickets to the trains anymore, so I got our bill stamped too."

"You took everything?"

"Yep. I thought I'd save you the trouble. Panther, Inc., can afford it. You ready for coffee?"

He'd brought coffee and sweet rolls from the hotel lobby. He laid it out on the table in front of the couch and motioned for Fortune to sit beside him as he spread out the maps and leaned forward. She began to relax. He wasn't paying any attention to her. He wasn't going to mention the underwear.

And he'd packed all the snacks.

Fortune suddenly felt good. He didn't understand her need to store the leftover food, but he'd done it anyway. And he hadn't teased her. She couldn't explain the quiet feeling of comfort that his actions had caused.

Plopping down beside him, Fortune didn't try to ignore the ever-present tingle that announced its presence as their thighs touched. He didn't seem to notice. It had to be her, and a response that was eroding her nerve endings with every touch. He simply spread his legs and leaned closer to the table. Fortune swallowed her breakfast without tasting it. For the first time in her life she drank an entire cup of black coffee without flinching.

The cowboy was wearing his snakeskin boots and his jeans, but he'd left off the leather, and the olive-drab T-shirt was fresh. She wondered what he'd done with his dirty clothes. She might have offered to rinse them out, but that would bring up a discussion of her underwear, the underwear she'd stuffed under her shirt when she'd heard his voice.

He'd combed his blond hair back away from his forehead. As it dried, it fell boyishly forward across his face. She couldn't resist the impulse and stretched her left hand out to push it back, caught herself, and for a moment her hand floated uncertainly, before she dropped it to the map, searching for some comment to justify its presence.

"Uh, Hunter, which way are we going?"

"What?" Hunter suddenly leaned back and turned, trapping the hand holding her sweet roll against the back of the couch. She rocked off balance and fell against him.. "Well, now," he said in surprise.

Fortune stiffened. She couldn't move. Somebody had got out the hammer again, except this time it wasn't nails holding her in place, it was invisible wires of magnetic energy.

With one swift motion Hunter slid his left arm under her bottom and turned her so that she was sitting in his lap with her map arm around his neck.

His blue eyes probed her dark ones.

"No," she whispered, as his head moved down.

"I think yes," he said as his lips found hers.

Holy hell, he was kissing her. His mouth was slanting possessively across hers, slowly, too slowly, as if he were deliberately trying to drive her crazy. He was assaulting every inch of her mouth desperately, as if he were a thirsty man who'd found a pool of water in the desert. He leaned back against the sofa. She went with him, melting against him, the heat of his touch dissolving her very bones.

There was a moaning sound. It might have been Fortune, or it could have been Hunter. There was no defining the sound, no holding back, no resistance to the raging fire between them. The parlor car seemed suddenly to sing, and their bodies took up the humming motion as though the rail car had started to move on its tracks. Fortune was moving. Hunter was moving beneath her. She could feel his burgeoning hardness throbbing against her bottom. Deeper and deeper the kiss went and the heat built, hands withdrew and forged into new areas until their skin was bare. They sizzled where they were touched.

Hunter twisted around and pressed Fortune against the seat of the couch, moving over her in a motion that stopped abruptly as he yelped and froze in place.

"Ohhhh, damn!"

Fortune blinked, suddenly aware of her surroundings, of Hunter, who was pressing her into the cushions beneath her body.

"What's wrong?"

"Nothing. Damn! Just be still for a minute." He rested his head against her cheek and took several shallow breaths. "Sorry, wild woman." His voice was hoarse, not from the depths of passion but from pain.

"I know," she teased, trying to gather her senses and cover her disappointment. "The spirit's willing, it's the body that's saying no. I think that I probably should thank your body."

"Somehow," he said with a gasp, "I don't think either of us would be honest if we did. And I never did believe in paying lip service to a lie."

With his arms he forced himself up sufficiently so that he could grasp the back of the couch. From there he was able to stand. Now he was pressing both his hands against his back.

Fortune shivered. Her tank top was around her neck, her exposed breasts aroused and throbbing. But it was Hunter who was in real agony. Quickly, she pulled her shirt down and stood up. Ignoring the obvious evidence of Hunter's desire, she moved behind him. "Get down flat on the floor, Hunter."

"Sorry, wild woman, if I get down, I may not get up again, and as much as I'd like to oblige you, I don't think I can handle it now."

"Lie on your stomach, cowboy. I'm going to work out those spasms. It's obvious that you haven't made any sudden moves lately."

Because he didn't argue, she knew how badly he was hurting. He knelt and stretched forward, grimacing as he lay down. "So, I'm out of practice. Does it show?" he quipped.

"Not this morning, but I got a good look last night when you went to sleep in the tub, remember? You gave new meaning to the phrase 'rise and shine.'"

She began to work her hands up and down his spine.

"Ah, yes. Well, there are ways of gaining respect and there are ways. A prune-shrunken body in a tub is not the best reference for a man, wild woman," he managed to say, biting back a grimace.

"There was nothing shrunken about you a

minute ago. As for prunes—hmm—I seem to remember I was eating a prune Danish when we got—uh—when you attempted to ravish me."

"You mean when you threw yourself at my poor body?"

"I did not throw myself, I was propelled. All I was trying to do was—" *run my fingers through your hair*, she almost said. Instead she said, "find our place on the map."

"I think that's what I've been trying to do for a long time, my lady with the magic hands, 'find my place on the map.'" Hunter let out a deep sigh and gave himself over to Fortune's ministrations. This time he let go completely, swimming in the gentle sensation of her touch, letting go any thought of control or conflict.

There was a harmony between the slow pulsing of the blood in his veins and the easy, quiet sound of her breathing. Tension drained out of his pores in a rush of heat, replaced by a sense of belonging that was strong and complete. Two people, their auras enveloped one with the other.

Fortune Dagosta was healing his body with her touch.

"We're on a sandy beach," Fortune was saying softly. "Remove every thought from your mind. Listen. Feel. The ocean is lapping gently on the shore. The sun is warm on our bodies. We're alone without a care in the world. Just you and me."

There was a long silence. "Listen to the water, Hunter, you can hear its voice. You can feel its warm touch, starting with your feet. Like the light of the sun, it moves up your body, warming it. Do you feel it? The light has reached the back of your knees. Your thighs. Your bottom. Your back. It's loosening, stretching. All the pain is being carried away by the water. The heat of the sun is bringing peace. The pain is gone."

She leaned back on her heels and waited.

Slowly, Hunter turned over and stared at her.

"What are you, Fortune Dagosta?"

"I'm nobody special, just a person who helps people."

Hunter was swimming in the emotion of the moment. For all his life he'd pushed people away, refused to allow anyone to get close. He hadn't needed anybody and didn't want that to be altered. Now, in the space of two days, everything had changed. He didn't know how it had happened, and it scared the hell out of him.

Confusion warred with the peace Fortune had wrought with her hands. Yet he wasn't ready to push away the peace, for the confusion was not born of anger but of something more powerful. Not just desire, but certainly desire was inborn in the feeling. Yet desire met compassion. Fear met . . . what emotion was he sorting out of this honesty? Love? No, Hunter Kincaid had spent his life avoiding love.

Fortune had given a little part of herself to him. But she gave little pieces of herself to anybody that needed it. If she were his, he'd stop that. If he ever fell in love, he'd want it all. He was selfish that way.

Anybody who shared his life had to close out everybody else. No runaways, no strays, no men with injuries to be nursed. He'd demand an equally selfish woman, a hard woman. And this five-foot dynamo who shopped at Goodwill might shoot sparks of fire at anybody who thwarted her, but she wasn't hard enough to ride with him. Even if he wanted her to, even if he could visualize that firm body beneath his without closing his eyes. He pushed away that thought. He had to break the spell.

"Apparently, I can't do much to stop you, wild woman," he said, and feigned a suggestive smile, "so if you'd like to have your way with me before the maids arrive, I think you'd better hurry. I've already checked us out."

Fortune's eyes widened.

The moment was spoiled. Their connection dissolved. She wanted to hit him. Every time his tenderness slipped out, he jerked it back with a vengeance and said something to drive her away. Another minute and she'd have forgotten about protection and gathered up the cowboy's little secret hurts and loved them away.

But he'd spoiled it, turned it into some little quickie on the bedroom floor. She stood up, letting the disappointment she felt sweep over her. He simply stared at her in return, his eyes as wide and open as a summer sky. Then she understood. He wasn't ready to be had—not like that. He was challenging her, closing her off in the only way he knew how, by reducing what he felt to pure sex.

Well, it wasn't going to work, not anymore. She'd learned his secret. He was looking for his place, just as she'd been. He just didn't know that he'd found it. She held out her hand. "Thanks, cowboy, but when I have my way with you, it'll be when you're as emotionally involved as I am—and prepared, which I'm not."

Hunter took her hand and came slowly to his feet. The pain in his back was gone, but his legs were weak and there was an ache in his middle that wasn't sexual. The feeling wasn't painful. On the contrary, it was oddly comforting.

Hunter busied himself refolding the maps. Fortune dressed, rescued her Danish from the back of the couch, and followed Hunter when he started out the door. At the parking area she snapped on her helmet and slid onto the back of the cycle. It was spotted with dried raindrops from a shower during the night, its fine coat soiled and worn, like her, like Hunter.

She touched the machine, feeling the warmth it had already absorbed from the morning sun. It didn't look quite so menacing. In fact, she was beginning to enjoy riding it.

Hunter started to get on, stopped, and extended his closed hand. "Here, you may need these." He opened his fist and revealed her lace panties, the ones she'd tucked beneath her shirt. They unfolded, draping over the edges of his big hand like the petals of a flower.

"I like the lace," he said, and planted a quick kiss on her startled lips as he swung his leg over the machine and started the engine. "White seems to be a contradiction to the pointed hair and bare feet, wild woman."

Fortune didn't answer. He was wrong, but she didn't know how to say it.

Hunter drove away from the Choo-Choo and found the freeway. He was sorry he'd said anything about the panties. He'd been sorrier that he'd found them. When he had walked into the bathroom to shower and had discovered them hanging so innocently on the tub, he'd been shocked. Their white lace seemed to be such a contrast to the fiery woman who wore them. He'd have expected red, or black, not bridal white.

It wasn't until they were on the outskirts of town that he remembered what Fortune had said about being prepared. He made a note to take care of that problem at their next stop. Hunter considered himself laid-back and easygoing. Few things bothered him, but there were some things he didn't take chances on. For he was past telling himself that he and Fortune weren't going to make love. He knew they were. It was just a matter of when.

"This is the one bad thing about riding a motorcycle—rain." Hunter rolled the bike off the apron on the freeway and sat beside Fortune on the slanting concrete abatement beneath the overhead highway.

"How long do you think it'll last?" she asked, rubbing her arms against the chill.

They were within an hour of the Bear Trap outside Nashville when the heavens opened up. The shower cooled both the air and Fortune's bare arms as they waited. Great drops of rain were hurtling down, plopping with such force, they bounced off the pavement and fell a second time.

"These spring showers don't usually last long."

"What would we do if we had two or three days of rain?"

"We'd either have to drive very slow and get very wet, or we'd lose. Here, put this on." He stood with surprising ease and walked over to the cycle, where he pulled her blue shirt out of the saddle-bags and draped it around her shoulders. "I don't think I can stand here and look at you."

She glanced down at her tank top and wished she'd replaced it with the T-shirt. She'd never thought much about what she wore. Her body was simply a part of her, and if looking at it brought somebody pleasure, so be it. But Hunter wasn't just anybody, and the pleasure took hold and made her aware of herself as she'd never been before.

"We might as well eat while we're stopped." Hunter took the small red-and-white cooler, opened it, and set it between them.

She slid her arms into the shirt and nodded.

"Cola, milk, or fruit juice?"

"Is there a sandwich?"

"Ham and cheese or roast beef. Which?"

"I'll take milk and roast beef."

Hunter handed her the food and carton of milk. He opened his travel guide and studied the map as he ripped the paper from his sandwich. "Damn!"

"What's wrong?"

"What day of the week is it?"

"Saturday, why?"

"Minnie Pearl's hat. How are we going to get it?"

Fortune frowned at him. "I don't know—we'll ask her for it, offer to buy it, steal it if we have to. What's wrong?"

"According to the guide, these other stars have some kind of gift shop or museum where they spend some time—except her. The only way we're going to get to her is at the Grand Ole Opry."

"So?"

"The Grand Ole Opry only takes place on Saturday night."

"So—" Fortune cut herself off. It was Saturday. They'd planned to get the postman bear first, on the chance that he was delivering a message they'd need. "If we go to the Bear Trap first, we might not get back in time to make the Opry. If we go to the Opry first, we could miss an important clue."

"And if this rain keeps up, we might not get to either one," Hunter said glumly.

"And we only have one Saturday night."

"Yeah, that makes everything a bit tight, doesn't it? If everybody has the same clue. Wonder how many hats Minnie has?"

Fortune swallowed the last of her sandwich, dug around in the cooler for the crackers she'd swiped, and ate them. "Well, I guess that means we'll just have to get wet," she said, stowing her paper in the trash bag and brushing off her hands. "I'm ready when you are."

"I know you're willing, wild woman, but we'll wait. I've already had one accident, I don't want to take a chance on having another, not with you along."

"Cowboy, if you were alone, would you go?"

"Probably, but I'm not alone." He leaned back on the slanting concrete and put his hands behind his head, as if he were going to take a nap.

"Hunter Kincaid, you get up. I insist that we leave now! I refuse to lose this scavenger hunt."

"Why don't you get the camera and take my picture. Get the rain in the background. If we lose by a few hours, I want to show the officials that it was because of an act of God."

"Do you think they'd accept that?"

"Nope, but it will give you something to do while we're waiting."

"I don't want to take pictures. I don't want to sit and wait. I want—"

"I want—I want—Come here, Fortune."

Hunter's eyes were closed. He wasn't watching. He wasn't arguing or paying any attention to her tirade.

"Sit down and talk to me. Tell me about your father."

"My father?" she asked suspiciously. "Why should I do that?"

"Why do you hate him so?"

"I don't. Or I didn't. He wasn't worth that much energy. I hated what he did to my mother."

"What did he do?"

"He worked her to death. At least that's what I thought. But I was a little girl, and a child's picture of things is sometimes distorted. She died when I was six, remember. After that he sent me to live with his mother."

"And your father? Where'd he live?"

"I don't know. He wandered in and out, until my grandmother died. Then he came back to claim what she'd saved."

"How old were you then?"

"I was sixteen."

Hunter opened his eyes and held out his hand. "I left home when I was sixteen too."

Fortune allowed him to pull her down beside him. "Not for the same reason, I'll bet."

For Hunter, Fortune's voice said it all.

"Did he—do something to you?"

"No—no, but he would have, sooner or later." Her answer was strained, and this time it was Hunter who shared Fortune's pain.

"You're right. I didn't leave for the same reason," he said, pulling her into the curve of his arm, gathering her to him, comforting her. "But there are other ways to be hurt. There's greed, fear, and there's the secret, terrible kind of love that damages people in the name of doing good."

"Does this have anything to do with a little boy smelling his dad's cigar smoke on the back porch, cowboy?"

"Yes, the memory and the man. Sometimes I have a hard time remembering what my father looked like. He stole that from me."

Hunter wasn't talking about his father anymore, but the man who'd adopted him.

"Why did your mother marry him, Hunter?"

"She thought that it was best for me, to give me a home and a father. At least that's what I always believed."

"And now are you having second thoughts?"

"I don't know. The man's a mystery. He never gives up. He just keeps on trying to make me a part of his world."

"Could it be that he cares about you, cowboy?"

"I can't imagine why. I don't understand why my mother is his champion. His children too. Julie and Penny seem to really respect the man. And my brother, Robert, does also, when he isn't going through the normal sixteen-year-old rebellion."

"The same kind of rebellion you went through?"

Fortune liked the feel of being close to Hunter. She liked the manly smell of him, mixed with the heat of the earth and the cool breeze that accompanied the spring rain. There were cars whizzing past not fifteen feet away, and yet they seemed hidden as the two of them lay back against the concrete.

"Maybe, but I ran away from home. Robert's still there. I guess I have to be honest and admit that says something about Robert."

"Or maybe about Hale?" Fortune asked softly.

"I don't know. I've spent some time thinking about that recently. I don't understand. After all these years a normal man would have given up. Hale still thinks I'm going to take my place in Kincaid Industries."

"You call him by his first name?"

"In my kinder moods."

"Yet something tells me that you're not entirely convinced he's the demon you believe."

"It's just that he keeps on trying to play the game. The man came to the hospital when I was hurt. He didn't tell me, but the nurses said he didn't leave until I came out of surgery and he was sure I'd be all right."

"Doesn't that tell you something?"

Hunter's fingertips were digging into Fortune's arm. She didn't have to be told that he was revealing more than he'd meant to.

"All it says is that he was keeping up the image of the Kincaid name. My mother wanted me to be safe, and he saw to it that I was taken care of properly. When the hospital was ready to release me, he paid the bill and sent the limo to pick me up and bring me home."

"And that bothers you, his paying the bill."

"No, it took every penny I'd saved, but I paid him back."

"What were you saving for?"

"It doesn't matter."

"Oh." But it did matter. He'd spent every penny he'd saved repaying his adoptive father. She didn't know what he'd planned to do with his savings, but that explained why he wanted the prize money. Fortune digested the information and felt a chill ripple over her, a chill that had nothing to do with the rain.

Rain? She sat up. The rain had stopped.

"Hunter, the rain has stopped. The sky is clearing. We can go."

Everything was becoming clearer, she decided, everything but the reason why he wanted the prize money. And she'd been trying to find a way to claim all of it.

"Well, wild woman, which will it be first, the bear or the hat?"

Fortune thought for a long minute. "The bear. There's something about that clue that intrigues me. If we don't get to the Opry, we'll find another way to reach Minnie."

The Bear Trap was busy, very busy. Fortune and Hunter looked at each other with surprise until they went into the shop and heard the sound of music. At the back of the store was a small stage where a band was playing. The man sitting on a stool was singing about the streets of Baltimore, and the crowd of onlookers were listening with rapt attention.

"Bobby's singing," the clerk said, "if you'd like to listen for a while before you look around."

"Uh, no thanks," Fortune said quickly. "We're looking for a postman bear. Would you have one in stock?"

The clerk smiled and nodded. "Sure do, right this way. There was a shelf of furry bears of all occupations—postmen, firemen, policemen. But the clerk went to the end of the counter, where there was a section of bears beneath a glass shelf. "Which one you want, hon?"

Fortune looked at Hunter, who nodded for her to

choose. She picked a small tan bear with bright button eyes and a summer postman's uniform with short pants. She quickly turned him around and examined his mailbag. Sure enough, in his mailbag there was a letter, a real letter addressed "To any person who has an imagination."

"Do they all have letters?" Hunter asked.

"The ones in this case do," the clerk answered. "They're special stock, not to be sold unless a person specifically asked for a postman bear."

"Open it, wild woman."

"Wait a minute, sir, you have to buy the bear first."

Hunter took a clip of money from his pocket and paid the woman as Fortune tore into the envelope.

"We're invited to a ball, Hunter, a charity ball for the children's hospital. I don't understand."

"Neither do I. Let's have another one of those bears," he said to the clerk.

"I'll sell you one," she agreed, "but they all say the same thing. I know. I put the notes and the ticket in the envelope and into the bear's mail pouch. I'm supposed to give you this too." She handed Hunter a second envelope.

Inside was money, a great deal of money, and a business card. "'Western Wear for all occasions,' the card says."

"Excuse me, ma'am." Hunter followed the clerk back to the cash register, where she handed him his change. "Do you know anything about this ball we're invited to?"

"Only that everybody in Nashville will be there. It's a western affair, a real high-class gala. They auction off objects donated by the stars."

"Like hats?" Fortune asked. "Like Minnie Pearl's hat?"

"Probably."

"And when is the ball, cowboy?"

"When else, tonight."

"Uh-oh, and what time is it now?"

Hunter looked at his watch. "Four o'clock. We'd better hurry. If we're going to spend this money for clothes to wear to a ball, we need to get moving."

"But if we spend the money on clothes, we might not have enough to bid on Minnie's hat."

"So we won't buy clothes, we'll rent some. Have you got a telephone directory we can use, ma'am?"

The Yellow Pages listed several stores where formal western attire could be rented. In less than thirty minutes they'd found one and explained to the clerk where they were going. He knew about the event, and after directing them to the dressing rooms began to bring out possible outfits.

Fortune couldn't believe the kind of clothing he was showing her. She'd never imagined owning such dresses. Finally, she settled on a copy of a slinky red sequined Barbara Mandrell dress with long sleeves and a high neckline trimmed with black fringe. It fitted her like a glove, and every bead moved as she breathed. The costumer added a pair of red satin evening shoes and glittery dangling earrings.

Hunter didn't comment on his choice when they met back at the cash register. When the clerk found out that his customers couldn't provide a permanent address, he lost his helpful manner.

"Sorry, the only way I'm allowed to rent our garments to people without a permanent address is with a deposit equal to the amount of the replacement cost."

"All right, how much?"

"A thousand dollars ought to cover it."

Fortune groaned. They were lost. If they left the deposit, they couldn't be sure they could bid on the hat. "Hunter?"

Hunter thought for a minute, then reached inside his wallet. "Maybe this will do it."

The clerk looked at the card and swallowed hard. "Er, yes, certainly, Mr. Kincaid, shall I have these delivered to your hotel, or will you want to carry them with you?"

"Send them," he said gruffly. "And they'd better be there in an hour." He took Fortune's arm and practically dragged her out the door.

"What was that all about?"

"Let's just say that part of Hale's determination is paying off. A long time ago he had business cards made up for me, showing that I'm an employee of the Kincaid Hotel chain. I've fought my name long enough, I guess I might as well use it. Buckle up."

"Where are we going, cowboy?"

"Where else, to the Kincaid Hotel."

"We are? Why?"

"Because that's where they're holding the ball."

Wisely, Fortune didn't asked any more questions. She knew that Hunter was in a rage. It was obvious that he resented having to use his name, but he'd done it. The question was why? It certainly wasn't to impress her. There were other ways to get to the ball, to get one of Minnie's hats. It had to be because he wanted to win.

And Fortune was beginning to think they might.

After all, they had six more days before the deadline, and only two clues left to solve. They already knew that the next location they were searching for was Lithia Springs. But the last clue, the mysterious reference to direction and a creature's tears, was still a mystery. Nothing in any of the books had offered an answer.

Maybe she'd call Lucy. Lucy might have an idea. Fortune wanted to check on the children anyway.

As soon as they walked up to the registration desk and Hunter identified himself, she knew what it meant to be with a Kincaid. In spite of the odd looks she received, the clerk fell all over himself to help Hunter.

It took some arguing from Hunter to make the clerk understand that they wouldn't accept free lodging and that they couldn't afford the presidential suite. Hunter finally settled on regular adjoining rooms, connected by a small foyer. The rooms proved to be so luxurious that Fortune wondered why on earth Hunter Kincaid hated the man who'd given him his name so much, he'd turn his back on all his wealth.

"The evening begins with a banquet at seven, followed by the auction and a dance," Hunter was saying.

"That's nice," Fortune said, still standing in the middle of her room.

"It's after six now. I suppose we'd better start getting ready. Do you have everything you need?"

"I think so, but then I've never been to an affair like this, so how can I be sure?"

There was a knock on the door. "Bell captain."

Hunter opened the door and let the hotel employee enter the room. He was carrying the costumes from the rental shop.

"Where shall I put these, sir?"

"In here," both Hunter and Fortune said, pointing at different bedrooms.

"Just lay them across the chair," Hunter said, "we'll sort them out. I guess you're nervous," he said to Fortune, closing the foyer door behind the bellman.

"I guess I am."

"Which bedroom would you like?"

"Either one."

Hunter took the bag containing Fortune's dress, and the accompanying boxes, into the room on the right. "If there's anything you need, we can have it sent up."

Like what? she wanted to ask. Nerve pills, a hairdresser, and a makeup artist. Maybe a maid to help her dress. Hunter wouldn't need help. She could tell from the ease with which he moved about the suite that he was far more used to living in luxury than she. She'd thought they were alike, birds of a feather. She'd been wrong. Every flower in the vase on her dressing table pointed out the difference between them.

Hunter might have run away from home when he was sixteen, but this was the kind of home he'd run from. She'd run from a house with no paint on the walls and dirt-filled automobile tires used as flowerpots along the driveway. Now he expected her to dress up in spangles and go to a fancy ball. She wasn't Cinderella.

Fortune nodded and walked quickly into her bedroom, closing the door behind her and leaning against it. Ten of her precious minutes evaporated before she was able to stop shaking long enough to turn on the shower. In the bathroom she found a shower cap, shampoo, and fancy soap.

Feeling slightly decadent, she stepped into the marble shower stall and adjusted the water controls. The shampoo was sweet-scented, as was the body gel. Even the towels smelled of cologne. By the time she discovered the hair dryer and container of makeup, she decided that there were advantages to being wealthy.

Fortune's usual sunny nature eventually took over. After a few giggles at her ineptness, she finally managed to pull on the pantyhose, the only article of clothing that the costumer clerk hadn't provided. Fortune sorted through the makeup and considered her objective. She might look like a street child normally, but it was by choice. One of her temporary jobs had been as a makeup artist for a burlesque house. She knew how to create beauty, and tonight she wanted to be beautiful.

By the time Hunter knocked on her door, she was wearing the red sequined dress, the satin high heels, and her most elegant uptown face. She picked up her black beaded evening bag, took a deep breath, and turned around.

The door opened, and Hunter was ready to chide Fortune about the lateness of the hour. He started to speak, but his throat closed over and caught his words behind a mountain of tightness. This time he didn't even try to hide his surprise. This time his laid-back air of acceptance whooshed away, leaving him absolutely stunned.

Fortune Dagosta was a vision.

Fortune Dagosta was beyond a doubt the most beautiful, alluring, sensual woman he'd ever laid his eyes on. And she was holding her breath in abject fear.

"Wild woman," he whispered throatily, "if you so much as look at another man tonight, I'll kill him."

"I shan't," she replied, drinking in the sight of her golden cowboy in a black tux, with a matching red cummerbund and bow tie, black boots with silver trim on the toes, and silver buttons on his shirt. "I promise. I won't even see another man."

For one long moment time quite simply stood still, then both Hunter and Fortune began to grin. "Damned if we aren't the best-looking couple I've ever seen. What do you say, Ms. Dagosta?"

"I say that I'm hungry, cowboy." Lordy, was she hungry. But food was the last thing on her mind.

"Yeah, but knowing you, I'd better order something from room service for later. These shindigs aren't known for good food."

"I think I like the idea of later," she whispered.

Hunter crooked his arm. "Then the sooner we leave, the sooner we can get back. Shall we go, madam?"

"Indeed, Mr. Kincaid. Do you have our ticket and our money?"

"Indeed, wild woman, tonight I'm totally prepared, *for anything.*"

Six

Fortune took one look at the banquet hall and changed her mind. She *was* Cinderella, and she'd come to the ball. Nobody knew who she was, and she doubted that any of the guests knew Hunter, but nobody ignored them.

A doorman in a tux took their invitation and motioned them inside. After a glance around the room Fortune decided her slinky red dress no longer seemed too extreme. She felt all eyes following them as she and Hunter found two empty seats at a table near the front.

Fortune remembered to pause to allow Hunter to seat her. Though she had about as much in common with these people as a hobo in Buckingham Palace, she felt pretty, and those staring people didn't know that she normally shopped at Goodwill.

"Close your mouth, darling," Hunter whispered in her ear as he pushed the chair beneath her. "Let them do the drooling."

Fortune turned her best uptown smile on Hunter as he sat beside her. She'd seen the country singers at the awards ceremonies on television and wondered at the blue jeans with holes in the knees, but there was none of that here. Sequins, satin, and elegance were the rule.

Across the hall she caught sight of the woman who'd worn the original dress from which hers was copied, Barbara Mandrell. At the same table was a very tall cowboy wearing a white western tuxedo. She kept waiting for him to turn his head. He did, and she recognized him as the star who'd gone on to make a fortune in the breakfast-food business.

Everywhere there were stars. Everywhere there were glamorous people wearing beautiful clothes, but she knew soon enough that many pairs of eyes were turned toward her and Hunter.

"There she is," Fortune said under her breath, "at the speakers' table."

Hunter followed her gaze. "Minnie Pearl, but she isn't wearing her hat."

"Tonight she isn't Minnie Pearl, cowboy, she's Mrs. Henry Cannon."

"Oh, I didn't know."

Fortune saw the very distinguished man sitting beside the elegant woman wearing the soft pink chiffon gown. She wasn't wearing her gingham dress and her hat with the price tag. Her face was both soft and beautiful, but even in this elegant setting, she was still Minnie Pearl.

A quick memory of her mother tugged at Fortune. She saw something of the same strength, the way she looked at night when they sat down to eat whatever food she'd managed to scavenge for her husband and child. But that was long ago, and the memory was gone and the woman she was watching was wearing pink chiffon instead of overalls.

The people sitting at their table introduced themselves, and waited expectantly for Hunter to identify himself and his date, but his only explanation was that he was Hunter and his lady was Fortune.

His lady.

Darling.

Loving words, lovingly uttered, and though she understood that Hunter was acting out a role, purely for effect, she wouldn't let herself be concerned with pretense. This was her night of nights. This night she was the princess. All she had to do was hang on to the prince. The only difference was that the object of their search wasn't a glass slipper but a hat.

The meal was served by black-aproned hotel employees who silently anticipated the diners' needs. Just before dessert Fortune was startled to find Hunter nudging her beneath the table. He was opening the clasp and sliding the last dinner roll inside her purse.

"For later, darling," he said softly. "Sorry, I don't think we can make away with any butter."

Fortune smiled and slipped her fingers beneath his jacket, massaging his lower back through his shirt. "How's the back, cowboy?"

"The back's fine, but my other parts are feeling neglected."

They weren't in the parlor car tonight, but they might have been. The clothes, the evening, the open awareness and promise of more were singing through their fingertips: his kneading Fortune's inner thigh; hers sliding down beneath the band of his briefs.

"Careful, wild woman," he growled menacingly, "you're about to start a range war, and this isn't the time."

Fortune felt her face flame as she placed her hand on the table. Hunter leaned forward and made some inane comment to the man sitting beside Fortune, then slipped his fingertips further between her legs.

"Hunter!" she said between smiling lips. "Stop that, right now!"

"All right, darling," he replied with a bland expression as he moved back to his normal sitting position. "For now."

They were saved from any further double-talk by the master of ceremonies, who stood and welcomed the guests. After introducing the sponsors of the event, he explained the purpose of the charity and brought on the guest auctioneer for the evening.

The first item was one of Clint Black's famous black hats that was quickly claimed for an astounding five hundred dollars. In the next hour goods were auctioned at an astonishing rate. Fortune was beginning to be alarmed. Suppose Minnie hadn't donated one of her hats, or even worse, suppose they didn't have enough money to buy it?

Finally, Minnie's hat was the next item up for bid. After a quick rush of offers there appeared to be only two people bidding seriously. The other man was across the room, and Fortune couldn't decide who he was. When the bidding reached a thousand dollars, Fortune began to panic. "Maybe we could explain to Minnie what we're doing, and she'd give us a hat," she whispered to Hunter.

Hunter didn't answer. Instead he stood. "Mr. Auctioneer," he said smoothly. "I do believe that Miss Minnie's hat is the prize of the night. In the interest of raising money for the children's home, I wonder if we might not let the gentleman bidding against me have the hat for the last bid—then, if Mrs. Cannon is agreeable, I'll match his bid for another hat."

The auctioneer looked startled for a moment; then, after speaking to Minnie, nodded enthusiastically.

Hunter sat down to the scattered applause of an audience that had no idea what he was really doing.

"You did it, cowboy," Fortune said, her voice filled with pride. "Five down and two to go, and we still have six days."

"And tonight, we still have tonight, my wild woman."

The rest of the auction passed in a blur of bidding. Fortune didn't know how much money was raised, but she knew that it had been a great sum. Enough to build a proper shelter for her runaways, enough to take in more. But she refused to think about that. This evening she was all dressed up.

This evening she had a ball to attend.

A side wall was removed, revealing an area for dancing. The guests were pushing back from their tables and making their way to the floor.

"Shall we dance, partner?"

"Oh, Hunter, I don't know whether I can even walk in these heels."

"Don't worry, I'll hold you up."

He put his arm around her waist and held her so tightly that she couldn't have slipped if she'd tried. They circled the speakers' table as the orchestra began to play. Fortune stopped, listening to the tune. She'd heard it before, earlier in the day, at the Bear Trap.

There were no words, but the song was clearly "Streets of Baltimore."

Hunter gathered Fortune in his arms. "Come here, wild woman, I've wanted to put my arms around you all night."

They danced. No, Fortune decided quickly, they simply held each other and the music caught them in its lovely sound and kept the rhythm of their hearts with its beat. Nobody attempted to cut in. Hunter would have swept anyone who tried away with a glance.

Only once did they part: she to go the ladies' room and Hunter to pay their bid. As she left the parlor, she had to wait for Hunter, who came hurriedly from the hallway, gliding to her side with such a look of longing that she sighed and leaned against him as if she were out of breath and needed to rest.

"It's almost twelve," he said, his blue eyes stormy with unspoken passion.

"And we've danced the whole night through."

"Not yet, wild woman, not yet."

He kissed her in the elevator, and again a moment later in the corridor outside their suite, pressing her against the wall. And then they were inside the foyer, still kissing, bodies shimmering with energy, faces flushed, eyes filled with yearning.

"Are you sure, wild woman?"

"Absolutely, cowboy."

His arms were around her back, clasping her loosely at her waist. Their breathing was quick and shallow, a vain attempt to bring cool air into lungs steamy with need.

Her hands were unbuttoning his shirt, sliding his jacket from his shoulders and pushing it behind to the floor. His shirt followed, and Fortune was able to lay her cheek against the golden hair on his chest.

"I've wanted to touch you here with my face since that first day. I love the feel of the hair on your chest, tingling like fire against me."

"Not fair," he said with a groan, "I don't have that advantage." He searched for the back zipper.

"No! Not yet." Fortune twisted away. She turned her face toward Hunter. "Kiss me again."

She stroked his face, reveling in the feel of him beneath her touch. His face was strong; his nose, his ears, all perfectly carved to match the stern look of him. This kind of touching was utterly new to Fortune. She'd never allowed herself to reach out to a man, not the way she was to him.

Hunter Kincaid, the loner, the rich boy who raced demon machines in obscure little places where screaming fans knew him as the Bounty Hunter, was very still.

His eyes were searching hers, searching as if he wasn't sure that he believed what was happening. There were questions. There was uncertainty. And she knew he wasn't a man who was ever uncertain about anything. Then he groaned and lowered his head.

He captured her lips gently at first, then more urgently, allowing his hands to caress her back, her shoulders, her breasts. The beads on the fabric pressed against her skin like hundreds of little fingers of heat. She moaned, giving herself up completely to the taste of his mouth, the bold intrusion of his tongue, the promise of wild, hot passion banked but blazing in the body of Hunter Kincaid.

Her hands left his face and sculpted the shape of his rib cage. Down through the downy chest hair they moved. She unfastened the cummerbund and his trousers, and pushed them to the floor, freeing the hard male part of him.

Fortune groaned. She was too short, far too short to match her need with his. Desperately, she slid her leg outside of his, taking his knee against the hottest part of her. When Hunter felt her arching to him, he pried his feet from his shoes, stepped out of the trousers puddled around his ankles, and backed to the wall, leaning against it.

Fortune felt herself begin to explode. Soon it would be too late to turn back. Maybe it already was.

"Fortune." Hunter pulled his mouth away. His voice was as ragged as his breathing. "Fortune, if you don't let me take off that dress, I'm going to rip it off, and that will cost us the prize."

"I'll do it." She gasped, flinging her head back so that she could see him. "Oh, cowboy, its . . .

It's—I can't even describe what I feel. Is it always like this, Hunter, between a man and a woman?"

"No, I don't think so. At least . . ." His voice trailed off as he looked at the woman he was holding. Her lips were swollen from his kisses. Her hair was tousled and shining like black coal in the firelight. She was riding him like the vixen in a man's most erotic fantasy, and she was openly acknowledging her desire.

He was on fire and he wasn't even inside her yet.

"No," he whispered, "it isn't always like this, at least it never has been for me."

"Hunter—"

The sharp knock on the door beside them seemed foreign. It came, stopped, and came again.

"Bell captain."

Hunter cursed under his breath and straightened his leg, letting Fortune slide to the floor. "You'd better take care of it, I don't think I'm dressed for guests."

Fortune stared at his nude body and shivered.

Then there was a click.

Someone was opening the door.

Fortune straightened her dress and stepped around the door to meet whoever was entering.

"Oh, sorry, ma'am. I was told that you were at the ball. I was instructed to bring this hat to your suite."

The bellman was standing in the light spilling inside from the doorway holding Minnie Pearl's hat. The ever-present price tag dangled from the brim.

"Thank you," Fortune managed to say. "I'm afraid I don't have a tip for you, but—" She knew she was stammering foolishly, but the thought of an aroused Hunter standing behind the door waiting had turned her stupid.

"No problem, it's been taken care of." The hotel employee held out the hat. Fortune took it and watched him back out the door and close it behind him.

"Lock the damned thing!" Hunter growled. He came out into the light, picked up his clothes, and pitched them across the sofa.

But the moment was shattered. Fortune's heart pounded in her throat. She couldn't believe her actions of a moment ago. She'd practically raped the man.

Hunter turned around, stared at her for a moment, and blushed.

Fortune had the absurd thought that he was providing a place to hang Minnie's hat. Then her eyes moved lower. His long, muscular legs were encased with very long, ribbed silk black socks. There was something incongruous about this nude man, this very hard nude man, wearing nothing but his socks. She began to smile.

"You think this is funny?" he asked. "You abuse me, arouse me, and stand there laughing at my poor hurting body while you're fully clothed?"

"Hurting body? Oh, I'm sorry, cowboy, I didn't think. I let you hold me up without realizing how painful that must be."

"My back would have to be riddled with knives to hurt badly enough to override what you've done to the rest of my body. Do something with that hat, wild woman, and heal me."

He stood before her, peeling his socks off and waiting, rocking back and forth on the balls of his feet.

She floundered, unable to answer or move.

"Fortune, you did this to me. I've been like this almost since the first time you crawled on that bike behind me. I want you. I need you."

She couldn't speak. The sheer magnificence of him overwhelmed her. The intensity of his gaze made her feel as if she were shimmering. There were invisible waves emanating from her body, covering the space between them like a heated coil.

All she could hear was the sound of their breathing. The ever-present tingling of her body was protesting in cadence with the throbbing of Hunter's proud signal of desire. Her breasts ached. There was a tender torture somewhere between her legs, and her pulse was racing through her body like a flood spilling over its banks.

"Please, my darling Fortune?"

She'd never know whether it was her own desire, or his calling her "darling," or maybe it was the "please" that did it. But just as she'd known earlier, there was no turning back. They were meant to be partners, and they were meant to be lovers. Fortune had always lived by her instincts, just as Hunter had. Now they'd found each other.

Reaching behind her, Fortune caught the zipper of the dress and lowered it, her eyes focused on Hunter with every ounce of her being. If this man was destined as her first lover, then so be it. The sequined dress slid from her body and made a splash of shimmering red around her satin shoes.

Hunter's breath quickened as the dress fell. Beneath it, Fortune's perfect breasts were free and standing out in passionate response to what was raging between them. She was wearing pantyhose, see-through hose.

She peeled off the hose and stood before him, more perfect than he'd ever dreamed. Hunter couldn't speak. His breath had left his body, and he was smothering in a wave of heat.

But it was her eyes that forced him to move. Black eyes that challenged, dared, lit up like those of a Spanish matador defying the mad bull in some fine old painting. He reached down to lift her.

"No!" she said vehemently. "We'll go together."

She took his arm, and they walked into his bedroom, where he pulled back the spread and pushed her down to the bed. He knelt on the floor between her legs and took her into his arms, whispering against her hair, "I want you to know that I understood what you were saying before, about not being protected."

Fortune jerked.

"No, Fortune, this is no thoughtless seduction. You're a woman who's made her own way, and I'm a man who's done the same. If we make love, it will be because you want it as much as I do. If that isn't true, say so now, and we'll stop."

Arms looped around his neck, Fortune swore softly. "Holy hell, cowboy, do you have to talk so much?"

Her heart was thudding so, she could barely talk. Why was he making her talk about what was happening? All she wanted to do was melt against him and feel. The warmth of his breath against her cheek, the touching of her nipples against his chest, sent exquisite waves of pleasure through her, and she trembled involuntarily.

Hunter stopped talking. His lips found other things to do as they moved down her cheek, tasting her skin, fanning little hot whirlpools of sensation, then moving down.

Lower and lower. He captured her nipple. Fortune moaned and leaned back, resting her weight on her hands on the bed, offering herself to him. Her lips were parted, her breath quick and uneven. The beginning stubble of Hunter's five o'clock shadow grated against the silkiness of her breast as he sucked her like a hungry babe.

And then she was falling across the bed, and he was falling over her, probing her, seeking entrance to that wild, hot part of her. He fumbled just for a second and raised himself over her, finding the place he sought, the place that seemed elusive, blocked.

He stopped, confusion stilling his movements. "What?"

Then Fortune arched herself against him and he was inside her, quivering on the edge of desire as she gave as much as he asked. No quiet, passive recipient of his passion, her hands and body were asking, demanding things of him that he couldn't refuse. Fortune was thrashing beneath him, thrusting against him, asking for more and more until they both hung together in a scorching shudder of release.

Fortune knew she was smiling as she felt him tremble once more, then fall across her with a groan of pleasure. "Cowboy," she began, searching for the words to express what she was feeling. "Was it, was I . . ."

"You were spectacular. But—why? Why didn't you tell me that you were a virgin?"

"I thought that you wouldn't believe me—that you'd think I was weird. I want you to know that I take full responsibility for this—I know what you must think of me—"

"Wild woman." He cut her off by turning over and pulling her into his arms and kissing her gently. "There are times, my darling wild woman, when we both talk too much."

It was much later when Hunter was still dealing with the responsibility he felt for the woman. His Mary Poppins of the pink bicycle, the woman who took in stray children and fought the justice system to keep them, had never made love to a man before.

He couldn't put that aside. He'd never experienced that phenomenon. Even his first time, when he'd been fourteen, hadn't been the first time for the fifteen-year-old "older woman" who initiated him into the world of sensual pleasure.

But Fortune Dagosta had been a virgin. She'd healed his back with her touch and his soul with her body. They'd been connected from the first, and now their lovemaking had sealed it. He'd stopped believing in forever long ago, but until after they'd won the prize, they were together, and it was good—very good.

He claimed her breast in his large hand and began to caress it. Her nipple swelled appreciatively, filling his hand as if it were saying yes, yes.

Fortune let out a soft sigh and found a place for her hand that Hunter approved of with a sigh of his own.

Later he carefully moved over her again and slid inside her. He knew he was a big man, and Fortune was so tiny. The first time, such a short time ago, had been shrouded in a haze of passion so intense that she wouldn't have felt the pain. This time he wouldn't take the chance that he'd hurt her. He supported himself on his elbows and looked down at her, half-asleep, flushed, and smiling.

The light in the entrance was still burning. In the half darkness he could view the dusky pink of her nipples, like ripe raspberries, the honey-color skin that made up the gentle curve of her small breasts as they peaked against his chest. Her nose was too thin, but it was impudent and matched her wide lips, which curved into an even wider satisfied smile. There was an errant strand of dark hair across her cheek that caught her long eyelash, giving her a seductive look.

Hunter felt himself throb impatiently as he tried to move slowly. She was still tight, though the ease with which she accommodated him freed his restraint, and he pushed himself deeper and deeper, slowly moving in and out until the sound of her breathing became as ragged and desperate as his.

She wanted him. Her body curved itself around him, demanding impatiently that he satisfy the need he'd aroused. Her lips were parted now, her legs spread wider as she lifted herself to meet him, writhing, bucking, her moans turning into little cries of need.

So sensitive to her body was he that he knew the moment it began, the rumbling, rolling announcement of her climax, overcoming her, drawing all tighter and tighter until she exploded, sensation rippling through her like a storm. And then he forgot everything but his own release, and they floated together in the afterglow of their loving. He rolled over, bringing her with him, as she continued to hold him inside.

Fortune lay, her face pressed against his chest, until he fell asleep. They remained joined, both physically and spiritually. She didn't want to move. She didn't want the night to end. She didn't want the light of tomorrow to change what they'd shared.

But like Hunter, Fortune knew that nothing was forever.

And she didn't want to lose the now.

The smell of coffee, and lips brushing hers, woke Fortune the next morning. She sighed and stretched, feeling the silky fabric of the sheets caress her naked body.

Naked!

Fortune sat up, winced, and grabbed at the covers.

"It's a little late for such modesty," said Hunter, making no effort to conceal his amusement.

"I know you're right, but—but—" She opened her eyes and glared at him. He knew how embarrassed she was, and he had no intention of turning away.

"I even swiped an apple off somebody else's breakfast tray," Hunter said solemnly.

"Thank you, but I'm not hungry. I'm . . ."

"What are you, then, my wild woman?"

"I think I'm sore, and I need a shower, and I need you to turn your back. You may be used to parading around nude before your paramours, but I'm not."

"Fortune, look at me. You don't have to worry. I'm not coming back to bed with you. We have to get moving. We still have the Lithia gold to locate, remember?"

"Yes, of course, and I have things to do. I'd like to call Lucy." She knew she was babbling, but she'd never been in this situation before, and she was nervous.

"Of course you may. Why would you ask?"

"I've been thinking about the rules of the contest. We aren't supposed to be using our own money, or family freebies, are we? I mean, couldn't our staying in your hotel be breaking the rules?"

"Not if we pay, and it isn't my hotel."

Hunter knew his voice was too sharp. But he wasn't nearly as settled about their relationship as he was pretending to be. He'd awakened early and spent an uncomfortable half hour feeling her pressed against him. The longer he held her, the more obvious it became that the previous night had not been a passing fling.

Finally, he'd separated himself from her, closed his ears to her sigh of regret, and left the suite. The desk clerk seemed surprised when he asked for his bill. It had taken a sharp reprimand from Hunter to force him to accept money from a Kincaid.

"I've paid our bill, except for your call. I'll get that on the way out."

"Do we have any money left?" Fortune hadn't thought about the cost of their night together. She wondered if it was too high.

"Enough to last the rest of the week, if we're frugal and if we don't have to attend any more balls. I'm going to return the rentals while you dress and eat," he explained, and gathered up the zippered bags containing the clothing. "Then we'll hit the road."

Fortune nodded and watched him leave the suite. He was back in leather again, once more the wicked Bounty Hunter. Now she knew why he'd been given that nickname. He'd caught her without a fight. She's surrendered herself willingly, wishing even as the door closed that he'd come back to bed and take her in his arms.

Lucy, she needed to talk to Lucy. Her explanation, that of asking Lucy if she could shed any light on the final clue on their list, was only an excuse. She wanted to hear from Joe. Fortune hoped that he'd come back.

Lucy and the children were still at Rachel and Tom's. She hadn't heard anything from Joe, though Rachel had put out a quiet inquiry among the places that teens often stayed. So far nothing had happened—except the health department had issued an injunction against Lucy staying in the house. It was unsafe.

The one bright piece of information that Fortune got from Lucy was that Panther, Inc., did not yet have a scavenger-hunt winner.

Fortune hung up, assuring her friend that although she and Hunter Kincaid were very close to solving most of the clues, the creature with tears in its eyes was still a complete mystery.

Lucy promised to do some research at the library. In the meantime Fortune could only hope the other teams had the same clue and were no closer to solving it than she and Hunter were.

Fortune was dressed and packed and waiting for Hunter to return. The ball gown and last night in Hunter's arms were beautiful memories, to be stored away and brought out in the quiet moments of her life, but they were only memories and should be treated as such. Reality was winning the scavenger hunt.

She heard Hunter's plastic card in the door.

"Ready, partner?"

"Ready," she said, and hurried past him into the corridor.

"Just a minute, Ms. Dagosta. You've forgotten something."

Fortune stopped and turned around. "What?"

"This."

He hadn't meant to kiss her. He'd planned to gather her and her pack and get started without rekindling the fire. But she looked so distant, so stiff, as if she were wearing new shoes and they hurt her feet.

But he was kissing her. And she was kissing him back, as the pack dropped to the floor between them. The thoughts of winning a scavenger hunt were lost as their lips touched.

Finally, Hunter pulled back. "Don't ignore what happened, wild woman. It's never happened to me either, and I sure as hell don't know what we're going to do about it, but we aren't going to ignore it."

"What's happened, cowboy?"

"I think we may have fallen in love, darling."

"No, I don't think so. I mean, I'd know, wouldn't I? Falling in love is a forever-after kind of thing, and I don't even know what tomorrow will bring. It's not possible."

"I know. It isn't. Maybe I'm wrong." He reached down, picked up her pack, and winced.

"Your back. Did we hurt it last night? I never even thought about it when . . ."

"My back is fine. My body is fine. It's a beautiful day, darling. Let's just go where the wind blows us."

"So long as the wind blows us toward Lithia Springs."

They mounted the bike and drove out of the Kincaid Hotel parking lot. Somewhere a church bell summoned early Sunday worshipers. As they rode out of town, the traffic thinned out. The sky was blue, the day was green, and the mountains were touched with pink. For two lovers it was spring, a lovely May morning. Suddenly, the day seemed fine.

Fortune slid her arms beneath Hunter's vest and squeezed him, pressing her face against his back. She felt every ridge of his body, his buttons, the pockets, the small round foil packets inside.

She suddenly blanched. They'd been so carried away that she hadn't even thought about protection. But Hunter had. Fortune felt her pulse flutter for a moment.

"What's wrong?"

Hunter's voice carried past the sound of the bike. He'd felt her body quiver. He'd felt her hands reach his pockets and stop. He'd meant to talk to Fortune about their being together, but everything was too new. He hadn't know how. In the past he wouldn't have been bothered, but this time he was.

Fortune merely shook her head and laid it against Hunter's back. How could she explain what his actions meant to her? How could she tell him of the times her grandmother had warned her against doing just what she'd done, loving a man. She'd used her mother as an example of what happened when a woman was weak. Fortune had believed her, watching her mother struggle to help pick crops in the field, make their meager earnings stretch to buy clothes and food for a little girl and a man who drank away a good portion of his salary every week.

Yet, her mother had loved her father. Even when she didn't have the strength to work anymore, she'd never refused him. Until the end when she'd finally had no more to give.

Fortune hadn't known what poor was until she'd been forced to live with her grandmother, who'd taken Fortune in and never let her forget what an inconvenience she was.

Now Fortune had let Hunter make love to her. No, not *let*, she realized, she'd met him thrust for thrust, kiss for kiss. Even now her body was giving out subtle reminders that it recognized and welcomed the attention of the man she was touching so intimately.

Fortune shuddered. She was learning that people could truly care for each other, and that loving could be very right. A blue-eyed cowboy with sun in his hair and heat in his loins had taken away all her resolve and left her wanting more.

Run away, that's what she ought to do. But she'd seen what happened to her children when they didn't face their troubles. They didn't run away from a problem, they simply carried it with them.

Truth was, she and Hunter were running together, through a spring day, toward a pot of gold at the end of a rainbow. She closed her eyes and gave herself over to the wonderful feelings rushing through her.

Seven

Hunter seemed anxious to get to the springs. They covered the distance back to Chattanooga by lunch, stopped for burgers, fries, and drinks at the take-out window of a local drive-in, and got back on the bike.

Fortune was disappointed when Hunter kept going. She didn't know how he was going to eat and drive, but she didn't doubt that he could do it if he wanted. She'd thought they might stop, talk a bit, and give his back a rest. He didn't explain his action, and she didn't ask.

There was an awkwardness between them that she didn't understand.

Then he pulled off the highway and drove down a gravel road. Minutes later they were beneath a stand of trees at the bank of the Tennessee River. Hunter killed the engine, kicked the stand in place, pulled off both their helmets and dropped them on the ground as he took her into his arms,

giving her the kiss she'd unconsciously been waiting for all morning.

"Lord, I've wanted to do that for the last hour,"
he said, his voice ragged with strain.

"I've wanted you to for longer," she confessed,
suddenly conscious that she was holding the take-
out bag, when what she wanted to do was put it
down and hold Hunter. "Let me get rid of this bag
and get off this bike so we can do it again."

He pulled back and looked at Fortune, at her
small, heart-shaped face, at the flush that highlighted her cheekbones and made her look as if she
were a little girl at her first circus. He put the bag
on the ground and half lifted her from the bike as
he continued to hold her.

"Let's find a place," he said, and turned toward
the river. The bag of food was forgotten as they
sank to their knees beneath the trees and stared at
each other.

"You know, this isn't smart, Hunter. Someone
might come by."

"No, I'm sure they won't."

"You are?" She gazed up at him, not realizing
how happiness colored her eyes. Instead of being
dark orbs of blackness, in the bright morning light
they were more like caramel, hot caramel, the kind
that burned your tongue with its heat.

He pushed her to the grassy bank and moved
over her, his fingertips touching her face, brushing back a strand of hair, as he caught her lower
lip with his teeth. He was shaken by the depth of
his desire, by his overwhelming need to be inside
her.

There'd been women, and he'd enjoyed a full
sexual life, but this was different. Making love to

Fortune was a fulfillment that felt so right, so complete. He'd been so careful, sensing that she was as concerned about the results of their love-making as he. Suddenly, everything changed. He never understood what commitment meant, until the thought of her carrying his child swept over him. But those kinds of thoughts were foolish; he couldn't be certain that her feelings were as strong as his. He wanted her to be a part of his life forever.

Now, looking at the desire in her eyes, he knew that she was as caught up in the moment as he. For now, it was enough. He pulled off her shirt and gazed at her breasts. "You're so very beautiful," he said, his voice husky.

"Beautiful? I'm too small, and my nipples are too big and dark for the rest of my—me—"

"Never hold back from me, wild woman. Talk to me, say what you feel, the way you make sounds when you're hot and ready to come."

Fortune blushed and turned her head to the side. "I do? I'm—I'm sorry."

"Don't be. Don't ever be sorry for feeling pleasure when I love you, for wanting me, for wanting to please me in return. That's what happens when two people are right together. That's the way it ought to be."

"But, I'm so—so—"

Then she lost the rest of her sentence as he took her breast in his mouth. She brought her hands up to thread them through his hair and hold him against her. *More*, she wanted to say.

"I thought you were hungry," she managed as he lifted her, and her jeans and panties went sliding down her legs.

"I am. This is what I'm hungry for, what I'm starving for, wild woman. What about you?"

"Oh, yes." She groaned as he stood and removed his pants.

"Oh, yes." From the pocket of his shirt he pulled the packet, tearing it open as he knelt beside her.

She watched as he held it between his fingers and rolled it over the length of him. Hunter was magnificent. She didn't know how he could possibly be interested in her, but he was. She wasn't silly enough to believe he'd meant the falling in love part. And as he lowered himself over her, she told him of her feelings with her eyes.

Fortune knew that if he'd forgotten the protection, she'd never have mentioned it. She was bothered by such a change in her thinking. All her life she'd known she'd always be careful about that one thing. No babies, no unwanted babies, no trapping herself or a man into a relationship that neither wanted.

Until now.

Now she understood total commitment—the forever kind of love.

Hunter was over her, the tip of him pressing against her, prolonging what was to come as if he were waiting for her to approve. She moistened her lips with her tongue and lifted herself to him, slowly, with trembling body and gasping breath.

What happened next was good and right and basic. It was a reflection of the emotion they felt, but it was more. It was a declaration of what was in their hearts. Their bodies brushed aside all thoughts, concentrating on the ascending rhyme of desire, building it higher and higher until they seemed to explode in a kaleidoscope of sensation.

"Wow!" Fortune let her hands fall to the earth beside her. She closed her eyes and took a deep breath. "I thought it would be—I mean I didn't expect—"

Hunter moved off her and lay on his back. "Neither did I," he said.

For a long time they didn't speak, each caught up in the wonder of what they'd experienced.

Then Hunter heard Fortune stirring. He opened his eyes. She'd come to a sitting position. There was a wrinkle in her forehead and a frown on her face. "What's wrong, darling?"

"Why did you call me 'darling'?"

"Does it bother you?"

"I don't know. Nobody but my mother ever called me that before."

There was a shadow across Fortune's face, a shadow that came with the mention of her mother. He didn't like that. Fortune ought always to be smiling. "Tell me about your mother."

"I don't remember a lot. She was beautiful to me, until she got sick. Then she got thinner and paler, and finally one night in a stinking little shack where the mosquitoes were the size of horseflies, she died."

"Ah, darling, I'm sorry."

Hunter took Fortune's hand and pulled her down beside him, capturing her head on his shoulder and her body in his arms. He wanted to hold her, take away the sadness.

Fortune continued. "My father had to take time off from work to dispose of me. He missed a good picking week while he took me to his mother's house and left me."

"Picking week?"

"My folks were migrant workers, cowboy. Peaches, oranges, grapefruit, strawberries. Whatever was in season. For a while after my mother died, my father came home when there was nothing to pick, and then finally, he didn't come anymore. Not until my grandmother died. Then he came to claim the farm."

"What happened?"

"He'd started drinking more and more. He didn't have any reason to stay sober. And then one day he realized that I was grown up. He—he finally decided it was time for us to get acquainted."

Hunter didn't have to ask what she meant; he could tell by the sudden stiffness of her body as she remembered. "The bastard!"

"Yes, but I ran away before he—well, you know."

Hunter tightened his grip. He couldn't take the memories away, but he wanted so badly to make it better. "I know how you must have hated him. I know what it means to lose someone you love. It's happened to me twice."

"But you still have your mother, Hunter."

"Yes, but she belongs to Hale now. No matter how hard I try not to resent it, I do. I'm beginning to understand that he didn't kill my father. But habits are hard to break. For so long, every time he touched my mother I wanted to hurt him."

The words tumbled out. For the first time in his life Hunter Kincaid shared his secret pain with another person. "My father worked for Hale, in the chemical plant. They made fertilizer. They made it the cheapest way possible. When he bought the plant, he'd been warned about safety measures.

Oh, he'd put in some new equipment, added some protective gear, but not enough. One night there was an accident. My father was killed."

"Oh, Hunter, I'm sorry." Fortune forgot her pain as she tried to assuage Hunter's.

"I was eight years old. But I knew the plant wasn't safe. The whole town knew. After that Hale closed the plant until he could correct the problems, but it was too late. Oh, he tried to make it up to me and my mother. The bastard gave her a job, moved us to Greenville, South Carolina, where Mother became his secretary."

"At least he tried to make it up to you, didn't he?"

"To me? I don't think so. It was my mother. Two years later he married her. It was a guilty conscience. He was a wealthy man. My mother was a simple woman. He didn't love her, I was sure of it."

"But he adopted you?"

Something about that decision bothered Fortune. The man had married Hunter's mother. Maybe he cared about her, maybe not. But adopting her son, making it possible for him to inherit the Kincaid family fortune, seemed unnecessary.

"Yeah, he couldn't have a kid around with a different name. That would mean explanations, and Hale Kincaid is a very proper man."

"But they're still married. And you have two sisters and a brother?"

There was a long silence. "Yes. I never understood that. I could almost see why she married him. She wanted to provide for me. But they slept together, made children together. And she's very loyal to him, even now."

"Did you ever ask her about that, Hunter?"

"Ask my mother why she slept with her husband?" Hunter's expression was one of incredulity. "Don't you think that's a little private?"

"Perhaps, but if you love your mother, and I think you do, maybe you owe it to her to try and understand. After all, she lost your father. Withholding your love seems like punishment to her as well as Hale."

Hunter didn't answer. He'd never thought about it that way. His mother always welcomed him home, and she'd tried to talk about Hale, make Hunter respect him and appreciate what they had. He hadn't listened. He'd done everything a boy could do to cause trouble for the man who'd taken his father's place.

But Hale Kincaid was a stubborn man. He'd refused to respond to Hunter's outbursts. When Hunter had got into trouble in grammar school, Hale had punished him and then put the incident behind them. When Hunter had refused an allowance, Hale had seen to it that Hunter had a part-time job that provided him with spending money.

When his sister Julie had been born, Hunter ran away for the first time. He'd been eleven. But Hale had found him and brought him home. That was the first time Hale Kincaid had really been angry with him. He'd made it plain that if Hunter didn't want to have a father-son relationship, he'd accept that. But his mother had just had a baby, and Hale wouldn't allow Hunter to spoil that for her by running away.

"Do you and Julie get along?"

"Funny thing about that, we do. She's everything that a man would want in his sister, except for her blind adoration of Hale. We don't discuss that."

"What about the other two?"

"I don't know. I was gone by the time they were born. Robert seems like a good kid, just what Hale wants in a son, I suppose. Certainly, he's more a Kincaid than I could ever be. I hardly know Penny."

"Did you ever try to please Mr. Kincaid?"

"Once. When I was sixteen, I actually took a job in the first hotel he bought. I actually enjoyed it. For a while I thought I might have been wrong about the man."

"What happened?"

"I *was* wrong. I ended up leaving home permanently."

"Hunter—"

"No, don't say anything, darling. Just hold me."

Fortune lay in Hunter's arms, holding him, wanting with every ounce of her being to take away the pain he was feeling. When it was obvious that he wasn't going to say any more, she turned her face and began planting kisses across his chest.

She found his nipples and felt them tighten beneath her lips. She slid over him, feeling the response of her nipples as they rubbed against his. She planted little wet kisses on the frown lines on his forehead, on his eyebrows, and down the side of his face. His skin was rough, his beard, though light in color, was already making its presence known.

Using her lips and her mouth, little by little she felt his tension ease, then rebuild in a different way. With little ripples it began, changing into subtle answering motions of response and soft moans of approval. She drew him away from the past and into the present.

Feeling her own shivery response, Fortune tightened her muscles, forming a circle of heat around the part of him that was shuddering as it stiffened.

"Fortune," he said with a groan. "Do you know what you're doing?"

"No, but I'm learning."

"But I don't—you said—"

"I talk too much, Hunter. This time I'm speaking in a different way. Just be quiet and listen."

And she took away his words with her mouth and his pain with her body.

Afterward he walked with her into the shallow part of the water. They cleansed themselves in the hot sunlight by the swiftly moving river; then, silently they dressed and ate their lunch.

Words seemed unnecessary. They felt a spiritual warmth that filled them and erased the last of their restraint. Fortune didn't know what would happen after the scavenger hunt was over, but she knew that her life was tied to this man's for as long as he wanted her.

Hunter sat beside her, touching her, feeding her cold fries, rimming her lips with his mouth, drinking in the touch and taste of her as if he were committing her to memory. Tomorrow was out there somewhere, but it was some hazy, distant unknown. He focused on now, which was more than he'd ever hoped for.

By four o'clock they were making the loop around Atlanta and heading toward Lithia Springs on the west side of town.

LOVE AND A BLUE-EYED COWBOY • 141

"According to the man at the service station, we take a right at Highway 278, and it's just down the road. There's a white fence, and we should be able to see the frog rock."

Fortune was more than ready to find the Lithia gold. Her back was aching and she knew that Hunter must be in agony. But more than that, her body was very tense. Holding Hunter, touching him, feeling him touch her most intimate parts, simply fed the fire inside her that seemed to burn constantly.

Nothing she did alleviated the growing anticipation of what the night might bring. She'd lost all fear. All she wanted was Hunter. She'd take him any way, for any amount of time, on whatever basis he said.

For the first time she understood why her mother had followed her father. Why Hunter's mother had shared a bed with Hale and given him children.

Children. What if Hunter had given her a child? She'd made love to him. She'd broken her most sacred vow, and all she could feel was joy. She shivered and snuggled closer, savoring the breathless feeling that swept over her.

The bike began to slow. The drive to the Lithia Springs Water Company loomed up, as did the large piece of granite that did indeed resemble a frog. At the end of the drive were several small buildings, including a turquoise wooden building with a lacy white postage stamp–size porch around two sides of it. The sign outside identified the building as the medical office of Christopher Columbus Garrett, date 1890.

Hunter parked the cycle and turned off the engine. It took a minute before they could stretch their legs and walk up the steps to the house.

"I hope there's still somebody here," Fortune said.

There was. A small, bright woman wearing a big smile invited them in, greeting them warmly. She was the proprietor of the springs, and on hearing their story, beamed even more.

"Yes, you've found the famous Lithia mineral water. It will definitely soothe your cares, and treat a few other problems too. This is what you want."

She handed them a small bottle of the water, packaged as Lithia Love Water, with the original label from the 1900s. "There were people who thought it was pure gold back then. And there are plenty who still do. I ship the water all over the world."

After a sales pitch for her mineral water and a quick history lesson on the springs, the woman let them go. She was more than happy to direct them to campgrounds near the springs where they could stay the night.

"Thank you," Hunter called out again, as they drove away. "The mineral water is the sixth clue, wild woman. But I don't know what we're going to do about the creature's tears."

"Maybe Lucy will have found something. She was going to the library today to do some research. I'll call her when we get to the campgrounds."

The campgrounds were located along a large, flowing creek. Following the usual commercial layout, there was a central office with a small store, a swimming pool, and separate areas set up for RVs, campers, and tents. Hunter picked a site along the creek bank, as far away from the other campers as he could get. They made camp for the night.

"Let's find the phone first and call Lucy," said Hunter, his voice as serious as a deacon at a funeral.

"And then?" Fortune had to ask, though she knew that his thoughts had to be following the same line as hers. Every time they'd touched, while they'd laid out the bedrolls, the tension had increased.

"Then, witch," he said with a growl, "then we shall see what we shall see."

"I see," she said very seriously.

"No, you don't, but you're going to." Hunter pulled her to him and gave her a quick, hard kiss that threatened to bring them immediately to a fever pitch.

She gasped. "The phone. The phone, remember? The creature with the tears."

"Hold that thought," Hunter said, and kissed her again.

"The fifty thousand dollars?"

"Ah—you know how to jerk a man back to reality." Hunter took her hand and pressed it against the hard part of him that needed her.

"Let's hurry, cowboy," Fortune said, and started toward the office at a run.

The pay phone was just outside the general store. Fortune got the operator and placed her collect call to Lucy at the prison farm.

But it wasn't Lucy who answered the phone. It

was Tom Benson. "Lucy left with Rachel to go into town. We got a call about your little buddy, Joe. He's in Orlando, in the hospital. He's been badly beaten."

"Oh, no. What are they doing?"

"Trying to work out something with the welfare office to get him home, or back here. But we don't have any way to move him, or a hospital willing to take him."

"I'll be there as soon as I can," Fortune said. "Where exactly is he?"

Tom passed on the name of the hospital with the message that Lucy hadn't found anything about a crying creature.

"Tell Lucy I'll call her when I get to Orlando. Not to worry. We'll figure out something."

Hunter was waiting impatiently. "What's wrong, Fortune?"

Fortune hung up the phone and turned to face her partner, the man she'd been ready to fall in love with, the man who'd claimed not only her body but an unretrievable part of her heart. The party was over. Cinderella had turned back into the scullery maid. The dream had ended. She was ending it now.

"It's Joe. He's been hurt. I have to go to him."

"The kid who ran away? Where?"

"He's in a hospital in Orlando."

"How bad is he?"

"We don't know."

Hunter hated himself for asking, and he already knew what her answer would be. "What about the scavenger hunt?"

"I'm truly sorry, Hunter, more than you'll ever

know. I need the money as badly as you, but there are other things that are more important."

"We could stop by the office in Cordele on the way down and sign in. We have six of the seven clues. Maybe we'll win on the shortest time, if nobody solves all the clues."

Fortune shuffled her feet. "No, I can't, Hunter. In fact, I was wondering if you'd let me have part of the money we have left to buy a plane ticket and rent a car. I'll pay you back. Nobody wants to accept responsibility for him. I just want— need—to get to Joe, quick."

"I see." He did. Joe needed her. Joe needed Fortune more than she needed Hunter. The woman fed on need, and it would always come first. What they had or were learning to have wasn't the forever kind of love. She was ready to throw away the prize money as well as him to go after some kid who'd run away, first from his family, then from Fortune. She was as stubborn as Hale Kincaid.

And without Fortune, Joe was as alone as he'd always been. But Joe had reached out for help. Maybe it was time Hunter did.

"Let me make a couple of calls, Fortune. Go back to the campsite and start packing. We're leaving tonight."

"But—"

"Do it, Fortune."

She didn't argue. When Hunter returned, Fortune had repacked the Panther and was sitting on the picnic table trying not to think about Joe. She was looking at her new tennis shoes and thinking of the undersize, frightened boy who'd run away because he'd accidentally set the house on fire, the little boy who wanted to see the Hemingway cats. He'd been hurt, and he'd never got to Key West.

She wasn't surprised. That was the way things seemed to work for Joe. All the wonder in life was just beyond his grasp. As it had been for Hunter. As it had been for her. She'd known all along that Hunter was a dream, that he was a temporary illusion in her life, that something would jerk him away from her.

The same way the scavenger-hunt prize had been. It had been within reach, and now it was gone.

"Let's move out, Fortune."

"Where are we going?"

"We're going to get Joe."

"We?" She felt her heart leap.

"We. We're partners, aren't we? Besides, I always wanted to see a cat with seven toes."

Fortune soon found that they weren't traveling to Florida on the Panther. Charlie Brown Airport, a small corporate facility, was within five miles of the campgrounds. There was a jet waiting for them, its flight plan already filed, the pilot standing by.

"How'd you do this?" Fortune asked, completely confused by what was happening.

"I didn't. Hale did."

"You asked Mr. Kincaid?"

"Yes. He made the arrangements. We'll fly to Orlando. The plane will stand by until we find out how bad the situation is, then we'll decide what to do."

"But, Hunter, you know that this means we've lost the contest." She was talking about the contest, but what she was really thinking was that Hunter had asked Hale Kincaid for help, and he'd provided it.

"Don't worry about the contest, Fortune. I'll find another way to accomplish what I intended to do with the money—to refurbish a fishing camp I inherited. Maybe I'll sell it and go to work in the hotel business. Hale will expect it after this."

They parked the Panther where the hangar owner indicated and boarded the private jet. In no time they were airborne and heading south.

Fortune stared out the window, her emotions skittering wildly. Hunter had called his father to help a boy he'd never met. Not only had she cost him the prize money, but he'd faced the man he hated, all for her.

"Why? Why'd you do this, cowboy?"

"Why'd you make love to me, wild woman?"

"Because you were hurting."

"And you wanted to take my pain away. Why?"

"I don't know. I just wanted to share it. Why'd you do this?"

"Because I care about you. What does it all mean, Fortune?"

"I don't have an answer." But she did. Suddenly, with absolute certainty, she knew. "No, that's not true. I think the answer is that I'm falling in love with you, Hunter. I never wanted it. I don't expect you to believe me, or to return my feelings, but that's the truth of it, cowboy. You burned my feet and singed my heart."

Hunter didn't respond. He sat in silence, listening to the whine of the engine in the night sky. His mind went back to the first time he'd seen Fortune, riding that pink bicycle with the wicker basket. She'd had her hair styled in little stiff points that made her look like a porcupine ready to attack.

And she'd been barefoot. She'd come to claim her spot on a scavenger hunt that required her to ride a motorcycle she was deathly afraid of, all to claim a prize to rebuild a roof on a house that had burned because of a runaway. Now the runaway was in trouble, and she was giving up her chance at fifty thousand dollars to answer his call for help. He'd never met anybody so giving.

He'd never met a woman who made him feel so good, so cherished. Yet she was throwing it all away for a sixteen-year-old who needed her more.

"You know what I was going to do with the prize money, Fortune?"

He hadn't called her "darling." Or "wild woman." He was talking to Fortune, and she wasn't certain that she wanted to be the person Fortune was. "No. You mentioned a fishing camp, but I don't know."

"My grandparents, my father's mother and father, owned a little fishing camp on the banks of the Flint River. When they died, they left it to me. I only found out about it when I turned twenty-one. By that time it had deteriorated until it was little more than a falling-down, screened-in porch attached to a shed. But it was mine. It was something that Hale hadn't provided. And I've hung on to it ever since."

"And you loved it."

"Oh, I loved it, but I couldn't stay there. I kept on moving. I couldn't be still, put my past behind me, and put down roots, even though I wanted to—so badly. I didn't tell you this morning, Fortune. But when I worked for the hotel, some money disappeared. I didn't take it, but Hale thought I did. He had me arrested, and I spent the night in jail."

"Oh, Hunter, I'm sorry."

"He thought it would teach me a lesson. It did. Don't trust anybody but yourself. I didn't take the money, but he thought I had. And it has taken me a long time to understand that he had every right to believe the thief was me. I'd certainly never tried to earn his trust."

Hunter reached up and turned out the lights, throwing the jet cabin into darkness. He was already opening up too much. The light was too revealing.

"Later the money was found," Hunter went on. "Somebody else was responsible. But by that time I was long gone. I never went back."

"Didn't he apologize?"

"Oh, sure. But that wasn't the point. He believed that I was guilty."

"It must have been very hard for him to let you stay in jail."

"But he never even asked me what happened."

Fortune took a deep breath and hoped that she was right in what she was about to say. "But, darling, isn't that what you did?"

"Me? What are you talking about?"

"Did you ever ask Hale about your father's death?"

"I didn't have to. Everybody knew he'd been responsible."

Fortune didn't answer. She'd said as much as she could say without appearing to take the enemy's side. But something told her that Hale Kincaid hadn't been any more guilty than Hunter had been. The problem was neither of them had known how to talk about his feelings.

She leaned her head against the back of the seat and closed her eyes. Her dream of having enough money to rebuild Lucy's house was gone. There was no reason to believe that the state would ever issue a license to her for her haven for runaways anyway. She didn't have the credentials to meet the basic requirements. As always, her dreams were bigger than her good sense.

Sports figures, famous people, they could raise money and open up homes for orphans and disturbed children. But not someone who had the same reputation as the children she was trying to shelter. Drifters didn't have clout. They didn't have money either. They shopped at Goodwill and worked as maids and waitresses or, sometimes, migrant workers.

No wonder the county had threatened to take the kids away from her. If it hadn't been for Rachel and her social work, they would already have done so. Dear Rachel, maybe she could arrange something for Joe. As for the others, there had to be an answer, a place. Fortune just hadn't found it yet.

She was very tired. For now she'd sleep and dream of a blue-eyed sun god who loved her pain away.

"There was a woman from Docket," she whispered, "who captured a seed in her pocket. The seed was a dream, an impossible scheme, but it flowered into love and she lost it."

Fortune Dagosta was back to covering her pain by spouting limericks.

Eight

There was a chauffeur with a black limo waiting as they stepped off the plane at the Orlando airport, who took them straight to the hospital.

Hunter inquired at the information desk, and they were escorted to the trauma unit. As they entered the cubicle where Joe was being treated, a tall gray-haired man rose from the chair beside Joe's bed.

"Hale?"

"Hello, Son, you made good time." He looked at Fortune. "The boy's still unconscious."

Fortune looked from Hunter to the worried man and back at her surprised partner. She slipped past them to the side of the bed where Joe was lying. He looked as if he'd shrunk even more. His small face was puffy and discolored, his eyes swollen shut, his lip split and covered with angry scabs.

"Joe? Joe, it's Fortune. How are you?"

He didn't move. He didn't respond.

"What—what happened—to Joe?" Hunter's voice was strained as if he had trouble focusing on the question.

"Tourists found him at a welcome station," Hale explained. "He'd been badly beaten."

"What does the doctor say?"

"He doesn't know. It could go either way. He might wake up in ten minutes, or maybe . . ."

"Never," Hunter finished the sentence in a whisper.

The nurse, waiting in the background, stepped forward. "I'm sorry. But only one of you can remain. Normally, we don't allow visitors to stay, but in the case of coma, we make exceptions. Hearing a familiar voice can hasten the patient's recovery. The waiting room is just down the hall."

"I'll stay," said Fortune, taking Joe's small cold hand in hers. "You two go, you've done enough."

Hunter started forward, but Hale's hand on his arm restrained him. Hunter turned back to face the man he'd considered his enemy for so many years, then allowed himself to be led away.

Fortune didn't even hear them leave. She sat on the edge of the bed, still holding Joe's hand. "Joe, can you hear me? Joe, wake up. I want to tell you about the scavenger hunt. I was picked, Joe. Thanks to you, we have a chance at winning all that money."

The sound of the machinery hissed and plopped in the silence. There were bubbles of liquid that released themselves at intervals. Somewhere beyond the half-walls of Joe's white cocoon there was someone moaning softly. The squish of nurses' shoes moving back and forth spoke of activity behind her.

Fortune continued to talk. Hours passed. Her voice grew hoarse. Hunter came in and urged her to take a break. She didn't even answer. If she could give enough of herself to Joe, she could bring him back. Finally, she felt her head drooping. She slid to the chair beside his bed, laid her face against his arm, and slept.

She was dreaming. From some faraway place Joe's voice came to her. She could hear him calling her, hear him as she strained to hear what he was saying.

"Fortune! Fortune! Wake up!" Joe's voice was louder. He was holding on to her arm, shaking her.

Fortune sat up. He really was calling her. Joe was awake. She felt tears of joy coursing down her face. He was all right. He wasn't going to die.

Behind her there was movement. Fortune turned her face to the intrusion. Hunter was standing there, misty-eyed and smiling.

"Good job, wild woman," he said quietly.

"Who's the dude, Fortune?"

"He's my partner," she said softly, "Hunter Kincaid."

"And this"—Hunter stood aside and allowed Hale to enter the cubicle and stand at the foot of Joe's bed—"this is Hale Kincaid, the man who got us here." Hunter couldn't call the man 'Father' yet. But after spending most of the night talking to him, he'd begun to realize that he might have been wrong about his adoptive father.

"Oh, my goodness," Fortune said apologetically, "I didn't even thank you last night. I was so concerned about Joe that I forgot all my manners."

"Don't worry, Ms. Dagosta, this night has brought me all the thanks I need. Now, young man, the nurses said that as soon as you came to, we could get you out of here and into a room. I'll bet you're hungry."

"You bet," Joe said brightly.

"What would you like to have to eat? Just name it," Hale said. "If they don't have it here in the hospital, we'll send for it."

"What I'd really like is some barbecue from the Creature House, but I'll settle for a Coke and some pizza."

"Is it really that simple?" Fortune asked with a worried frown.

But the nurse confirmed Hale's conclusion. Coma victims often woke up hungry and ready to go. Joe was out of danger, though his recovery was not yet complete.

It was the next day, after Fortune had slept most of it away, when the limo brought her and Hunter back to the hospital that she brought up what Joe had said about the barbecue.

"What did you mean by the creature house?"

"You never had any barbecue from the Creature House?" He eyed her with disbelief.

"No, I never even heard of it."

"It's awesome, Fortune, the best. There's this pig, this great big ugly pig on the top of the joint—at least it's supposed to be a pig, but it's so ugly that people call it the creature. And the barbecue sauce is so hot that the pig's crying real tears."

Fortune looked at Hunter.

"'The hideous beast,'" she said.

"'A tear from the creature's eyes'," Hunter said.

"What's going on?" Joe asked.

"Do we still have time, cowboy?"

"This is Tuesday. We have till Friday. Two and a half days. I don't know," he answered.

"Where is the Creature House, Joe?" Fortune asked, holding her breath.

"It's just over the Florida line, outside Tallahassee. You can't miss it, everybody knows it. Southeast Monster Meat is what the sign says."

"You can get there in a couple of hours," Hale said. "You can use the limo."

"No," Hunter said, shaking his head. "Fortune can't leave Joe."

"Sure she can," Hale argued. "I'm here. I'll stay until he's well enough to travel. Then he can go home with me. Your mother will have my hide if I don't bring him."

"I can understand that," Fortune said, looking at Hale Kincaid's relaxed expression. "But none of it matters, we can't go from here by limo. The contest rules say that we have to travel on the Panther, remember?"

"And it's in Atlanta." Hunter walked to the window and back.

"And we're here. I'm sorry, Hunter. I know how much winning meant to you."

"To you too. Look, we can still make it, wild woman. Hale, will you fly us back to Charlie Brown Airport?"

"Sure, the jet is on standby."

"If we don't have any problems, darling," he said, holding out his hand to Fortune, "we can pick up the bike, and maybe we can still get there. What do you say, shall we go for it?"

Fortune grinned. "There was a woman from

Bentz, who had absolutely no sense. When asked to fly, she said, 'I'll try.' She was not too hard to convince."

"You're right, Hunter, she's some woman," Hale Kincaid said, laying his hand on Hunter's shoulder. "Reminds me of your mother."

They climbed into the limo with Hunter charging the driver to hurry. Once inside, he pulled Fortune into his arms.

"No, Hunter, stop."

"Why, what's wrong?"

"I've had a lot of time to think in the last two days. I know that we've been caught up in a dream, but I'm not sure that we ought to let ourselves get carried away by it."

Hunter released her and leaned back. "What does that mean?"

"I don't know. I just know if you kiss me, we'll start making love, and maybe that's not smart."

"Oh, and why is that?"

"I mean, look at my mother. Look at your mother. They were both caught up in love affairs that hurt so many people."

"A love affair? You think that's what this is, an affair?"

"I wasn't sure until I saw you with your father this morning. But you've talked through your problem, haven't you?"

"Not completely. But yes, we've talked. I don't know if we'll ever have a solid relationship, but we have an understanding that we'll try."

"I'm glad. He seems ready to meet you halfway."

"I think so. And it's because of you. I found out a lot of things I didn't know. I found out that the plant where my father was working was sabotaged by union organizers. The workers didn't want a union. But some union sympathizers thought if enough bad things happened, the people would turn to the union to save them from unsafe working conditions. Something went wrong, and my father was killed."

"But why would you believe Hale now?"

"I was only eight years old, Fortune, but one thing I knew—my father was a union man. I went with him. I heard them talking about Hale Kincaid, about how Hale was against them, about how they planned to fix it so that Hale would have to let the union in."

"Oh, Hunter, I'm sorry, so sorry."

"I saw him leave that night. Nobody ever understood why he was in the plant. There was an explosion, and he was killed."

"And nobody was suspicious of his being there?"

"Hale covered it up, Fortune. He said that my father was working. He paid all his funeral expenses and took my mother and me to South Carolina so that I wouldn't find out."

"Why didn't your mother tell you the truth?"

"Hale wouldn't let her. He wanted to protect my memory of my father."

"So, now you'll go home and work with Hale, the way he's always wanted you to."

"Maybe, I don't know. Right now what we want to do is win that money. Lucy's house needs a new roof."

"Yes," Fortune agreed, more sure than ever that she'd made the right choice when she'd pushed Hunter away. He'd go home, where he belonged. But she didn't belong in his world. She'd never fit in. And Hunter would expect her to change. They'd shared something special, something neither had ever experienced. Together they'd erased all those years of hurt and bad feeling. They couldn't mistake that for love—not the forever kind.

He'd been her first lover, and she was still fascinated by his lovemaking. She understood that he'd credit her with his new relationship with his family. But she didn't want gratitude. She didn't want sex.

Fortune wanted Hunter's love, but she'd learned a long time ago that wanting was something she could live with. She'd also learned to move on when the time was ripe. That way she'd always have the happy memories. That way she wouldn't be hurt. That way she wouldn't lose the cowboy with the sun-god eyes.

The plane landed in Atlanta. They thanked the pilot and reclaimed their Panther. After consulting the map, Hunter handed Fortune her helmet and donned his own. By two o'clock they were heading south, back toward Cordele, where they'd started.

By six o'clock they were turning in the prison-farm gates. Lucy and the kids met her at the door with hugs and questions. While Hunter took a quick run back to contest headquarters to make certain that there wasn't a winner already, Fortune explained the situation to her friends.

"Yes," she'd answered, "Joe is going to be fine. Hunter's father is taking him to Greenville to Hunter's family home to recuperate from the beating he received. After that? Who knows. It depends on Joe, and the shelter."

"Why would anybody hurt Joe?" Mickey asked.

"The boys who beat Joe didn't know he was

broke. They wanted money, and when he didn't have it, they punished him."

"Surely, the authorities can find them," the warden said. "With Joe able to give them a description of the boys and the truck."

"They're looking," Fortune said, "but they haven't been found yet."

"Fortune, I'm sorry, but I couldn't find a thing at the library about any creatures with tears," Lucy said dejectedly.

"We think we have the answer," Fortune explained, glancing at her watch. "Joe solved it. It's a barbecue place with a big ugly pig as its logo. Apparently, the sauce is so hot that the pig cries real tears."

"All you have to do is bring back some of its tears, and you'll win!" Jade exclaimed with excitement.

"Then we can rebuild the roof and get a license and you'll have Fortune's House. We decided to name it for you," Beau said shyly.

But Fortune had heard the sound of Hunter's bike arriving. She stood up, gave everybody a good-bye hug, and ran down the walk to meet him.

Though Hunter seemed to be over his aversion to prisons since his talk with his father, she wasn't certain that he was comfortable about being behind bars.

"Has anybody claimed the prize, cowboy?"

"Not yet. One team gave up, took the bike, and left. One team had a wreck, and one team was disqualified. So far as the officials know, the other eleven teams are still in it."

"And we still have another day and a half," said Fortune, sliding behind Hunter. "Are we going to spend the night somewhere and go for the tears tomorrow, or keep moving?"

"I think we'll keep moving. We're too close to take a chance on something happening."

Too close. Hunter's words haunted Fortune as they left Cordele and took Highway 19 toward Albany and on to Tallahassee.

What did he mean by too close? He wanted to hurry and end the contest so that he could claim the money and they could part company? *They* were too close, not too close to the end?

She felt a pain somewhere in her throat. It swelled and tightened, threatening to close off her air. The miles seemed to fly by, and now she was torn between wanting to finish and dreading the end of the hunt. By the next day it would be over.

Holding on to Hunter, feeling the smoothness of the leather against her face, she felt like Joe's creature. Her head ached, and the tears spilled over her eyelids and wet the back of Hunter's vest.

The next day Hunter would take his money and be gone.

The next day the contest would be over.

She'd been wrong. This time she hadn't left in time. This time her memories wouldn't be happy ones.

It was late when they crossed the state line. Stopping by Lucy's had delayed them, but even Hunter had agreed that they should. Now they had to find the restaurant. Joe could only say that he'd stopped there after he'd accepted a ride with his attackers. But he was fuzzy about the location.

For more than an hour they drove around,

stopping, asking, until finally Hunter headed for the Tallahassee Police Department. He left Fortune outside while he went in. Instead of a spring in his step when he came out, he was walking slow, putting one foot carefully in front of the other.

"No luck?" she asked.

"Yes, I found out where it is."

"Then what's wrong?"

"Nothing, it's just been a long day."

That might be, Fortune decided, but it wasn't the entire reason for his dejection. "What is it, Hunter? Has someone beat us to it?"

"They didn't know. I just have a bad feeling about this."

"You're having woman's intuition? I don't believe it."

"I'm having—I don't know what I'm having!" He spoke sharply, swung his leg over the bike, and brought the engine to a loud roar, shutting out any further conversation.

"Are you sure you don't want to find someplace to sleep tonight and go there in the morning?" Fortune yelled over the noise.

Hunter didn't answer.

Hunter didn't know what was wrong. They were almost at the end. He knew that they were going to win. For the first time in his life he was going to accomplish something he set out to do. But the accomplishment was suddenly filling him with doubt.

He kept seeing Joe, bruised and battered. Joe who'd only wanted to see the Hemingway cats because they were freaks too. He thought of Jade and Beau and Mickey, all the ragged members of Fortune's little group.

He'd been like them once. But he hadn't found anyone like Fortune to stand up for him—not then. Now? He didn't know. Did he dare to trust her to return his feelings? Hale hadn't been what he'd thought. He'd spent so many years hating the man because he was afraid to know the truth. He'd taken the path of least resistance and had gone where the wind blew him.

Not Fortune. She'd stomped off into the sunset, a sneer on her face, her six-shooters drawn and ready for action. He was the Bounty Hunter, but she was the one who wrestled the world for what she wanted. He felt her arms around him, and he wanted them to stay there. He'd always told himself that if he didn't care, nothing could hurt him.

Now he was hurting.

The stars seemed to be congregating in the sky overhead. They'd left the city behind, heading back toward the Georgia line. At the proper spot he turned off the main highway and drove back into the woods, deeper and deeper, until finally he came to a stop.

The structure was dark, but even Fortune could see the large shape of an animal looming over the roof. There was the sound of water nearby, but she couldn't see the source. At that moment the moon vaulted out from behind the trees and hung there, a big, glaring silver-dollar moon that illuminated the shack, exposing the biggest, ugliest pig Fortune had ever seen.

"It's crying, cowboy. The water is from an artesian well, it's piped up to the pig's head and coming out of one eye like tears."

"'North is South and West is East.' That's it, wild

woman, *The hottest barbecue in the Southeast.* And here's our beast."

"I'll get the camera," said Fortune, hopping off the bike and plowing through the saddlebags. "Otherwise, they won't know we got the tears from the pig. Can you get up there?"

"I'll get up there, but how will we collect the tears?"

Fortune thought a minute. "The cooler. Are there any drinks left inside?"

"You mean those we swiped?"

"Yep. You see, you never know when you're going to need something."

Hunter nodded, opened the cooler, and emptied one of the cola bottles. He started toward the shack, studying the building while he tried to determine the best way to reach the roof. He'd told Fortune that he was fine, but his back had started to hurt long before they'd left Cordele. Now he was in quiet agony.

The tears were quite possibly worth fifty thousand dollars. But by collecting them, he would lose Fortune. He was having very mixed feelings about accomplishing their goal. But he didn't know how to stop. And he knew, too, that he didn't have the right. There were others involved, a motley group of teenagers who were homeless. Hunter walked to the tree beside the building and began to climb.

He stepped out on the roof at the base of the pig and stood while Fortune snapped several pictures. The quality was poor in the dark, but the judges would be able to tell. Nobody asked them to be photographers. He filled the bottle with water and climbed down, groaning as he jarred himself hitting the ground.

"Are you all right, cowboy?" Fortune came running to his side, sliding her arm around him.

"I'm fine. Let's go."

"Couldn't we rest now? I'm just worried about you, Hunter." Her voice was low as she turned and followed him slowly.

"Well, don't be. We've probably won. By this time tomorrow you'll have your twenty-five thousand dollars. You and Lucy ought to be able to get the house in shape with that."

"Yes," she managed, feeling the ever-present lump in her throat getting larger and larger.

Hunter stuck the bottle in the back, pulled on his helmet, and started the cycle, racing the engine impatiently as he waited for her to put away the camera and the pictures.

Perhaps it was because he was tired and driving too fast. Maybe it was because he was becoming more and more out of control. Fortune was leaning heavily against him. He thought that she was probably half-asleep, otherwise she wouldn't be plying her hands across his chest beneath his vest.

He could have stopped for a few hours. He knew he should stop to rest, but getting back to Cordele was all he could think about. And he almost made it. A few miles outside of town he increased his speed. He didn't know how it happened, but one minute he was flying down the highway and the next minute the bike was doing a cartwheel through the air.

"Holy hell!" was the last thing Hunter heard.

He was by the ocean, he thought. He could hear the water lapping against the shore. And the stars . . . He forced his eyes open, his vision blurring them into a smear of light overhead. And then he heard the silence. Not waves, but crickets and tree frogs.

He was in pain, dreadful, aching pain. Not just his back, but his shoulder as well. And someone was calling his name, over and over.

"Hunter. Hunter, please wake up. Hunter, are you all right? Please, my darling cowboy, don't die before I can tell you that I love you. Hunter."

Hunter blinked again, focusing on the face leaning over him.

"Holy hell, there once was a man who rode bikes, who thought he had some special rights, to drive like a fool, break all the rules, and kill himself one spring night."

"Wild woman," he whispered.

"Cowboy, you sorry excuse for a motorcycle racer. Can't you get where you're going without trying to kill yourself? Do you have some kind of death wish?"

"I never have before," he managed to say. "What happened to Florence Nightingale with the healing hands and gentle bedside manner?"

"She ran off with a bounty hunter. There's just you and me, kid. Do you think you can get up?"

"Maybe, but I don't think I can go anywhere if I do."

"You don't have to. I just want to get you on the Panther."

"Oh, Fortune. I seem to have a small problem with my arm. I don't think I can manage."

"I'll manage. I'll drive the Panther."

"You? But you don't know how."

"You showed me, remember? Anyway, I've watched

you for the last seven days. I'll manage. Wait right here."

Fortune had given the bike a quick look. It didn't seem damaged. Once again Hunter had gone in one direction and it had gone in the other, straight into a soft bank of dirt where he'd landed upright against the edge of a wheat field. She'd been slung into a stand of young wheat, which had cushioned her fall.

It still took Fortune a minute of struggling before she got the cycle turned so that she could roll it over to Hunter. Thank goodness they'd both been wearing their helmets. At least they hadn't suffered head injuries. Though she wasn't certain about Hunter. His eyes seemed a bit glassy.

Fortune straddled the bike. "Come on, Hunter, you can do it. Get behind me." She couldn't help him, for it was all she could do to hold the motorcycle steady. She started the engine as Hunter had showed her, praying that she remembered enough to get them into town, praying that the machine wasn't broken by the crash.

Hunter groaned as he came first to his knees, then struggled to stand. "Fortune, you can't do this. Let me." He took one step toward her and stumbled, almost taking both her and the bike down.

"Yeah, sure. Climb on, cowboy, this is my ride."

He followed instructions, collapsing heavily against her. "Use the clutch, wild woman, it's on the left."

Fortune reached back into her memory, and their earlier lesson came back to her. Get off the stand. Get in neutral. Put it in first, clutch, gas.

Even with her careful movements the machine

still jerked off at what seemed like fifty miles an hour. It was all she could do to get back to the road, weaving all over the highway like a drunk. Then she began to get the machine straightened out.

Clutch, second gear. Smoother, a bit faster.

Clutch, third, then fourth. And they were moving down the road.

She was doing it. They were going to make it. Please, God, she said, let me make it. I don't care if they put me in jail for driving without a license. If the children and I have to sleep in tents on the river, we'll do it, if You'll just let me get us to town.

"Hold on, cowboy, don't you let go. We're going to make it. Hold on!"

Hunter tightened his grip. He wasn't quite sure what Fortune was doing. The only thought that he held on to was that they were together. Wherever they were going, they were together. He wouldn't let go. He'd never let go.

At the hospital they had to pry his hands apart to get him into the emergency room. He had no head injury. Hunter was simply half-unconscious from shock and pain. He'd dislocated his shoulder and injured his back. After his shoulder was taken care of, his arm was put into a sling.

The staff insisted that Fortune be examined, poking, examining, intent on torturing a person who already knew that she was all right. When he released her, the emergency-room doctor gave her a stern warning to get a good night's rest.

Fortune called Hale Kincaid and told him what had happened. Joe wasn't ready to be moved yet, but Hale promised to be in Cordele by morning. Fortune sat by Hunter's bed until he was resting comfortably. Then she hitched a ride to Lucy's house with an officer who was a friend of the warden.

Later, alone and still shaken, she spread blankets under the stars and lay there thinking about what had happened. They'd lost the scavenger hunt. There would be no fifty-thousand-dollar prize. The lovely fairy tale was over, and it was time that Cinderella got back to the scullery.

The idea of Fortune's House, a no-questions-asked shelter for runaways, was only a dream. Even if she'd won the money, there was no guarantee that the community would accept the children. Already licensing boards and health departments were throwing stumbling blocks in the way. She felt a tightness in her chest.

Not only was Fortune's House a lost dream, but so was Hunter. "We're falling in love," he'd said. But that could never be. His dreams weren't the same as hers. His dream was a private one, separating him from the world. Hers took the world straight on and spit in its eye.

Still, she couldn't stop thinking about him, and how strong he was, about how he made her feel, and how alone she was without him. Being alone had never mattered before. Loneliness had been a way of life for her—until now. She sighed and closed her eyes.

She'd been alone before.

She'd be alone again.

She just wished she'd left the party earlier, when she'd been having the most fun.

Before she'd fallen in love.

• • •

The sun was high in the sky when she heard it, the sound of a car driving up Lucy's drive. Tom, she thought, probably coming to check on her at Lucy and Rachel's insistence. Fortune left the barn and started back through the rose garden toward the house.

But the car was a limo. It was a limo carrying Hale Kincaid and Hunter.

"Hunter, what are you doing here? Your back? Your shoulder?"

"Get in, wild woman," he said slowly, a glint in his eyes that dared her to disagree.

She complied. "What are you doing?"

"*We're* winning a scavenger hunt, you crazy woman." He pulled her inside the car and to the seat beside him, sliding his good arm around her."

"But you're supposed to be in the hospital."

"I know. And I will be, at least I'll be in bed, just as soon as we collect your money."

"*My* money? You crazy man, the money's half yours."

"I don't need it," he said, every word an effort. "The Kincaids are loaded, remember? I've decided that all Fortune's children need shoes."

Fortune felt her heart swell. The crazy man was worried about her kids. Because of them he'd made up with his father. Because of them he was willing to forfeit the prize and take a chance on injuring himself permanently. She couldn't speak—not even a limerick came to mind. She simply kissed him.

Before Hale, the driver, and anybody else who

happened to be driving down Fifteenth Street in Cordele, Georgia, she kissed Hunter Kincaid and settled back in his arm with a heart filled with joy.

They retrieved the cycle from the hospital parking lot. With great effort and obvious pain Hunter cranked the engine and, followed by his father in the limo, he drove to the dealership parking lot, where they presented their clues. They'd solved them all. They'd completed their task in less than the allotted amount of time. They'd triumphed.

But they'd come in second.

Early that morning, while Hunter was disentangling himself from the weights and pulleys that held him in traction, while Fortune had been sleeping the restless sleep of one whose heart was hurting, another team had driven in victorious.

Second prize was fifteen thousand dollars.

Second prize would put a new roof on the house and repair some of the damage, but half that much wouldn't. Still, it was a start.

"Thank you, Hunter," Fortune said, ready to shake hands and let him leave. She'd find a way to manage with the money she'd won. She wasn't certain how she'd exist with half a heart, but that was all she had left.

Half a heart and memories of how close she'd come to the forever kind of love.

"You take the Panther, Hunter. I could never drive that thing again."

"You did drive it, wild woman. You actually got us here on the Panther."

"I don't know how. I still think it's some kind of robo-monster with wheels. I'll stick to my pink bicycle."

"No problem, the pink bicycle is already loaded. We'll come back for Lucy and the kids," Hunter was saying with a grimace. His face was turning white, and his breathing was growing shallow. "I think you'd better get me to the limo, Hale."

Hale Kincaid stepped forward and supported Hunter on one side as Fortune walked beside him on the other.

"Where are you going, Hunter?"

"You mean where are *we* going?"

Hale helped Hunter into the car, stretched him out on the long seat, and held the door open for Fortune. "I don't think he ought to be alone, Fortune. And it isn't family he wants now."

As if in a fog, Fortune got in the car, kneeling beside the prone body of the man she loved. "What's going on, cowboy?"

"Remember that fishing camp that belonged to my grandfather?"

"Yes, on the Flint River."

"Well, Hale and I decided that it would make a much better shelter than it would a fishing camp. I have a confession to make, darling. I don't know one end of a boat from another."

"Shelter? I don't understand."

"Well, let's put it this way. There was a wild woman from Dover, who took in kids who were rovers. She fell in love with a dude whose father was glued—with connections and money all over."

"Glued?"

"Well, that's the best I can do when I'm in such great need of comfort and medical attention. Where are those wonderful hands, Nurse Fortune? Come to think of it, the rest of you can help too."

He reached down and pulled her onto the seat with him.

"Hunter, you're in great pain. You should be in the hospital."

"Not without you, wild woman. Never without you again."

Epilogue

The Flint River cut like a gray-green plow through ancient trees that bowed their branches in silent subservience to the water. Bright sunshine dappled light through the lush growth.

Beneath one very tall live oak, a man lay on his stomach on a blanket. His face was pressed against one folded arm, the other encased in the sling beneath him.

"Doesn't it hurt your shoulder for you to lie on your arm?" Fortune asked as she plied her fingertips down his back.

"Ummm."

"Is that a yes?"

"No, that's a ummm. Lower, Fortune."

Fortune slid her body lower, catching the back of his knee between her legs as she moved down.

"Ummm, that's nice. I hear the water lapping against my body. I feel the heat on my calf." He moved his leg from side to side. "Definitely hot, moist heat, I'd say."

174

"Hunter, stop that. It's bad enough that we're out here without our clothes. Don't—don't—"

He continued to move his leg against her, encouraging the moisture, igniting the heat.

"I'm trying to work the kinks out of your back, darling. Stop trying to start something."

Hunter stopped moving and turned over slowly, protecting both his shoulder and his back. He'd spent the last three weeks under Fortune's care, camping out in the remains of the fishing camp, cooking on an open fire, sleeping in her arms. There was still pain, but he was getting better.

"I think it's time we do some serious talking, my wild woman."

Fortune leaned back on her heels and waited. She'd known that sooner or later Hunter was going to get to his point, and she didn't know what she was going to say. He'd insisted that she have all the money. On one of his visits before he left, Hale had told her that Hunter had agreed at last to take a job with Kincaid Hotels. So she knew that no matter what plans Hunter had, their time together was limited. She'd accepted that.

She was prepared to let him go. She'd been away from Lucy and the children long enough.

"Fine. Serious talk, cowboy, you start."

"Not with you up there and me down here. Come down beside me, darling."

"Ah, Hunter. You know what will happen if I lie down beside you. That will last about thirty seconds and then—"

"Fortune! I need you here."

And she needed to be there. Quickly, she came to his side, into his arms, into the curves of his chest and waist, where her body fit instinctively.

"Fortune, in a few days there will be crews of construction workers swarming all over this camp, rebuilding, laying out facilities, and constructing new buildings. If it were up to me, there'd never be anybody here but us, but it can't be that way. You're a woman of the people, and if I'm going to share my life with you, I'm going to have to be a people person too."

"I don't understand."

Hunter took his hand and placed it gently against Fortune's cheek. "You opened a door for me, a door back to my family. I'm not certain yet that it will work, but I'm going to give it a try. What I do know is that whatever happens, we're going to build Fortune's House right here on the bank of the river."

"But I didn't do anything, cowboy, except fall in love. And I never meant to do that. The children are my responsibility, not yours. And I won't let them ever be a burden to anybody."

"I know." He stroked her face, rimming her lips, running his fingers down her neck and capturing her nipples. "You'd be perfectly willing to leave me and never let me know that you're going to have my child, wouldn't you?"

Fortune gasped. "Your child? What are you saying?"

With his good arm Hunter turned Fortune over and pulled her forward against him, taking her nipple in his mouth.

Fortune winced. Her breasts were tender. She stared down at herself in disbelief. She'd attributed the changes she'd been feeling to their having loved each other too much in the three weeks they'd been on the river, even though she'd thrown up the last three mornings. Reality came crashing over her. They'd been together for more than a month. And she was late. She hadn't even realized. And she'd never in her life been late.

Wide-eyed she stared down at Hunter.

"No. That can't be true. You used something. At least I thought you did."

"I did. But nothing's foolproof. Apparently something happened. It's true, Fortune. We're going to have a baby."

"A baby?"

"No, Cinderella, *our* baby. Don't you see, darling? We belong together. We've made a child together. And I'm going to love it as much as I love you."

Fortune couldn't gather her thoughts. A baby. The one thing she'd never expected to happen had. "Thank you, Hunter," she managed. "But you don't have to marry me. I never intended to marry. I never intended—holy hell! I don't believe it."

"Fortune, since that first night we've made love over and over again, and we've taken precautions. But you're carrying my child."

"We've been foolish. We should have thought about what might happen."

"No, we're incredibly right together, Fortune. Our bodies knew it. But more than that, so did our hearts. From the first time you tried to massage away my pain, I knew how much you could care."

And you bought me new clothes and you cared about Joe, she wanted to add. "But how is it possible?"

Hunter swapped nipples, giving the second one the same gentle loving that he had the first. Then he turned Fortune to her back and slid over her, supporting himself with his good arm.

"Because we're alike, Fortune. We're two renegades, hell-bent on taking on life alone. Just think what we'll be together. I'm going to do special assignments, public relations for Kincaid Hotels and its newest goodwill venture, Fortune's House. Ah, darling, you've given me life and a future. Let me give something back."

"Oh, Hunter, I wish—I wish . . ."

"I'll make all your wishes come true, my darling. I'm Fortune's Hunter, and we have our whole lives ahead of us. We might not have won the scavenger hunt, but our prize was forever after."

"Forever after," Fortune whispered, and felt the tight little knot of pain deep inside begin to unfold. She was opening herself up to the man who'd given her so very much.

"There was a young woman whose love, took flight on the wings of a dove. She flew wild and free, but her lover could see, that her heart fit his like a glove."

"There are other parts that fit even better," Hunter said with a chuckle.

And he was right.

THE EDITOR'S CORNER

The coming month brings to mind lions and lambs—not only in terms of the weather but also in terms of our six delightful LOVESWEPTs. In these books you'll find fierce and feisty, warm and gentle characters who add up to a rich and exciting array of folks whose stories of falling in love are enthralling.

Let Joan Elliott Pickart enchant you with her special brand of **NIGHT MAGIC**, LOVESWEPT #534. Tony Murretti knows exactly what he wants when he hires Mercy Sloan to design the grounds of his new home, but he never expected what he gets—a spellbinding redhead who makes him lose control! Tony vowed long ago never to marry, but the wildfire Mercy sparks in his soul soon has him thinking of settling down forever. This book is too good to resist.

Fairy tales can come true, as Jordon Winters learns in award-winning Marcia Evanick's **GRETCHEN AND THE BIG BAD WOLF**, LOVESWEPT #535—but only after he's caught in a snowdrift and gets rescued by what looks like a snow angel in a horse-drawn sleigh. Gretchen Horst is a seductive fantasy made gloriously real . . . until he discovers she's the mayor of the quaint nearby town and is fiercely opposed to his company's plan to build new homes there. Rest assured that there's a happy ending to this delightful romance.

Terry Lawrence's **FOR LOVERS ONLY**, LOVESWEPT #536, will set your senses ablaze. Dave King certainly feels on fire the first time he kisses his sister-in-law Gwen Stickert, but she has always treated him like a friend. When they're called to mediate a family fight at a romantic mountain cottage, Dave decides it's time to raise the stakes—to flirt, tease, and tantalize Gwen until she pleads for his touch. You're sure to find this romance as breathlessly exciting as we do.

Janet Evanovich returns with another one of her highly original and very funny love stories, **NAUGHTY NEIGH-**

BOR, LOVESWEPT #537, for which she created the most unlikely couple for her hero and heroine. Pete Streeter is a handsome hellraiser in tight-fitting jeans while Louisa Brannigan is a congressman's aide who likes to play it safe. When these two get entangled in a search for a missing pig, the result is an unbeatable combination of hilarious escapades and steamy romance. Don't miss this fabulous story!

You'll need a box of tissues when you read Peggy Webb's emotionally powerful **TOUCHED BY ANGELS,** LOVESWEPT #538. Jake Townsend doesn't think he'll ever find happiness again—until the day he saves a little girl and she and her mother, Sarah Love, enter his life. Sarah makes him want to believe in second chances, but can her sweet spirit cleanse away the darkness that shadows his soul? Your heart will be touched by this story, which is sure to be a keeper. Bravo, Peggy!

Spice up your reading with **A TASTE OF TEMPTATION** by Lori Copeland, LOVESWEPT #539, and a hero who's Hollywood handsome with a playboy's reputation to match. Taylor McQuaid is the type that Annie Malone has learned only too well never to trust, but she's stuck with being his partner in cooking class. And she soon discovers he'll try anything—in and out of the kitchen—to convince her he's no unreliable hotshot but his own man. An absolutely terrific romance.

On sale this month from FANFARE are four fabulous novels. National bestseller **TEXAS! SAGE** by Sandra Brown is now available in the paperback edition. You won't want to miss this final book in the sizzling TEXAS! trilogy, in which Lucky and Chase's younger sister Sage meets her match in a lean, blue-eyed charmer. Immensely talented Rosanne Bittner creates an unforgettable heroine in **SONG OF THE WOLF.** Young, proud, and beautiful, Medicine Wolf possesses extraordinary healing powers and a unique sensitivity that leads her on an odyssey into a primeval world of wildness, mystery, and passion. A compelling novel by critically acclaimed Diana Silber, **LATE NIGHT DANCING** follows the lives of three friends—sophisticated Los Angeles women who are busy, successful, and on the fast track of romance and sex, because, like women everywhere, they hunger for a man to love. Finally, the ever-popular Virginia Lynn lets her imagination soar across the ocean to England in the historical romance **SUMMER'S KNIGHT**. Heiress Summer St. Clair is stranded penniless on the streets of London, but her terrifying ordeal soon turns to passionate adventure when she catches the glittering eyes of the daring Highland rogue Jamie Cameron.

Also on sale this month in the Doubleday hardcover edition (and in paperback from FANFARE in May) is **LADY HELLFIRE** by Suzanne Robinson, a lush, dramatic, and poignant historical romance. Alexis de Granville, Marquess of Richfield, is a cold-blooded rogue whose dark secrets have hardened his heart to love—until he melts at the fiery touch of Kate Grey's sensual embrace. Still, he believes himself tainted by his tragic—and possibly violent—past and resists her sweet temptation. Tormented by unfulfilled desires, Alexis and Kate must face a shadowy evil before they can surrender to the deepest pleasures of love. . . .

Happy reading!

With warmest wishes,

Nita Taublib

Nita Taublib
Associate Publisher/LOVESWEPT
Publishing Associate/FANFARE

FANFARE

Now On Sale
New York Times Bestseller
TEXAS! SAGE

☐ (29500-4) $4.99/5.99 in Canada
by Sandra Brown

*The third and final book in Sandra Brown's beloved TEXAS! trilogy.
Sage Tyler always thought she wanted a predictable, safe man . . . until a
lean, blue-eyed drifter takes her breath, and then her heart away.*

SONG OF THE WOLF

☐ (29014-2) $4.99/5.99 in Canada
by Rosanne Bittner

*Young, proud, and beautiful, Medicine Wolf possesses extraordinary
healing powers and a unique sensitivity that leads her on an unforgettable
odyssey into a primeval world of wildness, mystery, and passion.*

LATE NIGHT DANCING

☐ (29557-8) $5.99/6.99 in Canada
by Diana Silber

*A compelling novel of three friends -- sophisticated Los Angeles women with
busy, purposeful lives, who also live on the fast track of romance and sex,
because, like lonely women everywhere, they hunger for a man to love.*

SUMMER'S KNIGHT

☐ (29549-7) $4.50/5.50 in Canada
by Virginia Lynn

*Heiress Summer St. Clair is stranded penniless on the streets of London,
but her terrifying ordeal soon turns to adventure when she captures the
glittering eyes of the daring Highland rogue, Jamie Cameron.*

☐ Please send me the books I have checked above. I am enclosing $_____ (add $2.50 to cover
postage and handling). Send check or money order, no cash or C. O. D.'s please.

Mr./ Ms. _____

Address _____

City/ State/ Zip _____

Send order to: Bantam Books, Dept. FN, 414 East Golf Road, Des Plaines, IL 60016
Please allow four to six weeks for delivery.

Prices and availability subject to change without notice.

THE SYMBOL OF GREAT WOMEN'S
FICTION FROM BANTAM

Ask for these books at your local bookstore or use this page to order.

FANFARE

On Sale in March

THE GOLDEN BARBARIAN

☐ (29604-3) $4.99/5.99 in Canada
by Iris Johansen

"Iris Johansen has penned an exciting tale. . . . The sizzling tension . . .is the stuff which leaves an indelible mark on the heart." --Romantic Times
"It's a remarkable tale you won't want to miss." --Rendezvous

MOTHERS

☐ (29565-9) $5.99/6.99 in Canada
by Gloria Goldreich

The compelling story of two women with deep maternal affection for and claim to the same child, and of the man who fathered that infant. An honest exploration of the passion for parenthood.

LUCKY'S LADY

☐ (29534-9) $4.99/5.99 in Canada
by Tami Hoag

"Brimming with dangerous intrigue and forbidden passion, this sultry tale of love . . . generates enough steam heat to fog up any reader's glasses." --Romantic Times

TOUCHED BY THORNS

☐ (29812-7) $4.99/5.99 in Canada
by Susan Bowden

"A wonderfully crafted, panoramic tale sweeping from Yorkshire to Iceland . . . to . . .London. An imaginative tale that combines authenticity with a rich backdrop and a strong romance." -- Romantic Times

☐ Please send me the books I have checked above. I am enclosing $ _____ (add $2.50 to cover postage and handling). Send check or money order, no cash or C. O. D.'s please.

Mr./ Ms. _____

Address _____

City/ State/ Zip _____

Send order to: Bantam Books, Dept. FN, 414 East Golf Road, Des Plaines, IL 60016
Allow four to six weeks for delivery.
Prices and availability subject to change without notice.

THE SYMBOL OF GREAT WOMEN'S FICTION FROM BANTAM

Ask for these books at your local bookstore or use this page to order.

FN28 - 3/92

FANFARE

FANFARE

Sandra Brown

_____ 28951-9 TEXAS! LUCKY .... $4.50/5.50 in Canada
_____ 28990-X TEXAS! CHASE .... $4.99/5.99 in Canada

Amanda Quick

_____ 28932-2 SCANDAL .... $4.95/5.95 in Canada
_____ 28354-5 SEDUCTION .... $4.99/5.99 in Canada
_____ 28594-7 SURRENDER .... $4.50/5.50 in Canada

Nora Roberts

_____ 27283-7 BRAZEN VIRTUE .... $4.50/5.50 in Canada
_____ 29078-9 GENUINE LIES .... $4.99/5.99 in Canada
_____ 26461-3 HOT ICE .... $4.99/5.99 in Canada
_____ 28578-5 PUBLIC SECRETS .... $4.95/5.95 in Canada
_____ 26574-1 SACRED SINS .... $4.99/5.99 in Canada
_____ 27859-2 SWEET REVENGE .... $4.99/5.99 in Canada

Iris Johansen

_____ 28855-5 THE WIND DANCER .... $4.95/5.95 in Canada
_____ 29032-0 STORM WINDS .... $4.99/5.99 in Canada
_____ 29244-7 REAP THE WIND .... $4.99/5.99 in Canada

FANFARE

Rosanne Bittner

_____ 28599-8 EMBERS OF THE HEART . $4.50/5.50 in Canada
_____ 29033-9 IN THE SHADOW OF THE MOUNTAINS
$5.50/6.99 in Canada
_____ 28319-7 MONTANA WOMAN .... $4.50/5.50 in Canada

Dianne Edouard and Sandra Ware

_____ 28929-2 MORTAL SINS .... $4.99/5.99 in Canada

Tami Hoag

_____ 29053-3 MAGIC .... $3.99/4.99 in Canada

Kay Hooper

_____ 29256-0 THE MATCHMAKER, ... $4.50/5.50 in Canada
_____ 28953-5 STAR-CROSSED LOVERS .. $4.50/5.50 in Canada

Virginia Lynn

_____ 29257-9 CUTTER'S WOMAN, ... $4.50/4.50 in Canada
_____ 28622-6 RIVER'S DREAM, ... $3.95/4.95 in Canada

Beverly Byrne

_____ 28815-6 A LASTING FIRE .... $4.99/ 5.99 in Canada
_____ 28468-1 THE MORGAN WOMEN .. $4.95/ 5.95 in Canada

Patricia Potter

_____ 29069-X RAINBOW .... $4.99/ 5.99 in Canada

Deborah Smith

_____ 28759-1 THE BELOVED WOMAN .. $4.50/ 5.50 in Canada
_____ 29092-4 FOLLOW THE SUN .... $4.99/ 5.99 in Canada
_____ 29107-6 MIRACLE .... $4.50/ 5.50 in Canada